COLD LAKE ANTHOLOGY
2024

Cold Lake Anthology 2024

Burlington Writers Workshop

Cold Lake Publishing

Contents

In loving memory
Sharon Lopez Mooney
1942-2024

From the Editors

The river is constantly turning and bending and you never know where it's going to go and where you'll wind up.

—Eartha Kitt

No man ever steps in the same river twice, for it's not the same river and he's not the same man.

—Heraclitus

A river winds through this book. It bends with each new page, flowing over stones worn smooth, crashing down waterfalls, carving ever deeper into the landscape. The river is time, and we are borne along. But we are also the river, changing the world as we pass through it while the world changes us. We are altered by bumps in the road, the joys and agonies of aging, destruction and creation all around us, and of course, the people we love. Though these currents can be fast or slow, gentle or violent, they are ever-present and eternal.

The sun rises in Whit Humphreys's "Still," setting the scene for our journey. In Ann Fisher's "The Rapids in Suburbia," the river eddies and erodes, changing the house and the body in which one dwells. Sally Ballin considers the source, showing how the tales we pass down evolve with each teller, in her nonfiction piece "The Story of Marmalade."

In "Mourning Dove," we pause for a moment with Bill Pendergraft to listen and find connection through birdsong. Time marches on, sometimes stopping us in our tracks, as in David Hinkhouse's "Roadblock," but we keep on running, along with Guorong Zhu in "Chicago Marathon: Run for Those Who Can't," and, closing out our collection, we find a rhythm in "An Alluvial View" by James Wyman. And so we meander on . . .

As you take in the stories and poems in this year's anthology, we hope that you find pieces of them to take with you on your journey downstream.

Nancy Volkers
Amy Place
Janet McKeehan-Medina
Amy Quenneville
Kimberly Kurzawa

Whit
Humphreys

Still

Breathe in, winter sunrise, and hold.
Exhale slowly earth and sky hues.
Undo night's cloak, light the sumac and dogwood
so the sun can weave cattails and fog
into a pink silken robe your morning will want to wear.

Jeff Bernstein

An Embarrassment of Senses

I.

Driving south out of the misty mountains
after visiting our daughter,
you tell me the only thing absent
from your happiness right now is our son,
away on the left coast. I know
what you mean, recall fecund lemon tree
in his backyard where I sat in April.
I inhaled pale sweetness of California
light, watched his little dog loll in lush grass,
product of once-a-generation winter rains
that painted super-blooms across dusty
mountains in spring. I picked a single fruit
to perfume my trip back to Vermont.
I did not want to let it go.

II.

I did not want to let it go,
that rain-spattered trip to Edinburgh
decades ago, we found the stop we'd needed
quite by accident, no GPS, no internet.
A tiny Scotch bakery appeared replete
with flaky sausage pies, rolls and shortbread
cookies shaped like Gromit (as in Wallace &).
We crossed the street as a few rays of sun
sliced the overcast—such relief to be walking
rather than driving on the left, sleep-
deprived as we were. You opened the door to
an aromatic cloud of yeast, chose cookies
from the display case for our small kids,
the temporary absence a dull ache.

III.

The temporary absence a dull ache,
missing the comfort of flowers until
you discovered lilacs we didn't know we had,
downhill at the cabin we call the Studio,
though the spiders, or fear of them, kept you
from painting there. Growing up, I picked
sprigs of lavender-colored blossoms
at the top of our crumbling driveway, placed them
in water-filled mason jars and sold them to
tolerant relatives as *lilac perfume.* I don't think
they gave any aroma at all. I never tried to

replicate my days in that line of work.
What would it be like to make a living
as purveyors, producers of sweetness?

IV.

Purveyors, producers of sweetness,
every sense primed, they take their positions
in the kitchen, noses up, hope in their eyes.
We've learned that berries are fine treats
but grapes and alliums are verboten.
After breakfast the dogs snuffle together
on the colorful mat where I hide kibble.
Outside, our young spaniel puts her liver-
colored nose to the ground, searches and
tests every manner of vegetation, critters and
insects. Yesterday she froze when a garter snake
almost touched her, soughing across the high grass.
The air hangs heavy between storms.
The woods on a rainy day beyond riches.

V.

The woods on a rainy day beyond riches.
We only recognize a small percentage
of what the canines read. They sense
that gray fox is somewhere in the upper
meadow. Do they see it, smell it (*Vulpes*

vulpes), hear it, or all three? Synesthesia of

cross-species connection. They study openings
in the high grass, wait for something to appear, chess

players working the board for the right move.
Cinnamon and ozone aren't half bad and
as we pass raised beds, basil's on the breeze.
The rosemary I cut is just sharp enough.
Even with clouds draping the meadow,
willowy light lingers past bedtime.

VI.

Willowy light lingers past bedtime.
Fireflies appear in the growing
darkness. I can just make out
the scent of lightning before
the first flashes scar the valley,
dogs begin to quake, smell fear
anticipating the cacophony that
soon will shake these ancient mountains.
I put my face beside the older
of the two, her right foreleg
palpably trembling, signaling
sensory overload of the highest
magnitude while sultry breezes
transport a mélange of spices.

VII.

Transporting a mélange of spices,
citrus, mint and rose ignite the roadside
wildflowers in late afternoon. The first golden
poison parsnips open, beckon like sirens.
Their oils burn with abandon on a sunny day
at the slightest touch. Passing the garden,

I can't help but taste the spicy arugula
and Black-Seeded Simpson lettuce that love
these thunderstorms, bathing in some endless
wash and wear cycle. Grass grows before my
eyes, steam rises the way fog rolled off
the ocean in my former life. Not the summer
we wanted, but the one we have,
driving south out of the misty mountains.

Ann Fisher

The Rapids in Suburbia

careening toward ninety
slowly, here on Llandrillo road
we discover ourselves unnavigable—

underneath number three-seventeen
age sinkholes each of our foundations—
so many silted years centrifugal

eroding

loss floods momentum
leaving the kitchen
our one sure eddy

where sediment kicks loose
floats downstream
over floorboards and stairs

memory-slicked, dangerous
aging's tug and pull
faster just below our surface

Ann Fisher

i am no supernova, no titan at birth —

more like a bag of groceries changing hands
than a star twenty times the mass of the sun

but i've made the best of my adopted aggregate
grew up short and small most un-star-like, really

so many millions of miles
and degrees of difference

still, we hold one phase in common
twins born of turbulence

this casting off and diminishing
in a halo of gas and dust

i am at my most luminous now,

exploding into sixty—

i've lived neither fast nor hard
like those massive stars

though i've burned my fair share
of darkenings and brilliances

we lose mass now at a higher rate
and aren't my arrowed attempts

to fuse memory and words
a star's bright bid to prevent collapsing?

is it too much to hope then,
that my cast-off flecks

my infinite cosmic grains
will sluff and gravity outward,

create the perfect dust-tote
for future molecules to gather?

Candelin Wahl

What Waits

That summer of her dying
     whip-lashed old losses   hobbled me
Grief dug her den like a twitch-tailed tigress
     under my ribs   claws sheathed
Days dragged into blind nights
     without her moon   I drew the drapes

By March I wandered pine woods
     flashes of red-white tail   tracks in snow
Pointed away from burrow to meadow
     waited and breathed   four paws bounced
High as a spring-loaded acrobat
     like first sight of trillium   that mama fox

Candelin Wahl

Scraping By: A haibun

Stepped into spattered painting jeans—they still fit after four years of COVID and condo life. Put on pink tee splashed with Sherwin-Williams *Buttery Yellow*—three former kitchens wore this. Arrived at a rental property, punch-list in hand. Laid out tarps and tools to scrape and paint porches, railings, original balusters. My fingers slid into a back pocket—crinkle of cash! Three one-dollar bills survived their last wash-dry cycle.

worn denim
sweat and blisters
scraping by

Sally Ballin

The Story of Marmalade

My dad was a writer—a poet and a storyteller. Sometimes his stories were true and sometimes, we kids later realized, they were wild embellishments or entirely his invention. The story of how oranges reached the bleak British Isles, from which he hailed, with the sinking of the Spanish Armada over four hundred years ago is one example. The notion that crates of that strange fruit bobbed ashore on ocean currents was one of those stories that didn't quite have the ring of truth, looking back on it. But that the English turned those oranges into marmalade had a curious authenticity because cutting things up and boiling them down into mush is indeed the cuisine of my ancestors.

However, the story of what marmalade meant to my family results from my father's harsh Victorian childhood in Somerset County, England, on that very coastline, and decades later, in America, his purchase of a single tree in an orange grove in Naples, Florida. When the annual shipment of bitter oranges arrived every January, the tiny kitchen in our Georgetown townhouse morphed into a marmalade factory for two solid weeks. Our dad's marmalade was legendary.

Typically, his relationship to the kitchen was limited to making ice for chilling martinis and making porridge for breakfast on Saturday mornings. But in January, he commandeered the resources of the household and tended a fragrant cauldron of burbling oranges, lemons, and sugar. Condensation trickled down the kitchen walls, the air pungent with the intense aroma of boiling citrus. My sisters and I were put to work slicing orange rinds and cutting out wax-paper discs to place atop the cooled brew once it had been poured into wide-mouth pint jars. We slaved at this work with waning enthusiasm as the mountains of oranges and hot steaming jars kept reappearing, evening after evening, on the dining room table. We would come home from school to the moist, sticky fragrance and know what tasks lay ahead for us.

Years later, I learned that his was a secret recipe, handed down from the monks of Cleeve Abbey where not only crates of Seville oranges but also several Spanish sailors had indeed washed up on the English shore and were taken in. The monks put those hapless sailors to work in the kitchen, perfecting a marmalade recipe that Queen Elizabeth I is said to have enjoyed when she had occasion to pass through the region.

My dad inherited the recipe from his family's cook who made marmalade for that household. How she came by it is not known, but my sisters and I are now the trustees of this secret and where it goes from here. Today's lifestyles don't provide for a family museum or archive. We no longer live on large estates with libraries, portrait galleries, and the artifacts of our ancestors. We have condos with barely room for the photograph albums, a few treasures from the family home, some favorite recipes. That's all.

But we also have stories whose origins we never knew or have forgotten, and we don't know the difference between fact and fiction, merely the lore that passes from one generation to the next, without verification and with each teller's embellishments. And so I share this story with you. Where lies the truth, I can't say.

Edward Baran

Song Against the Tribes
of Men

This recently discovered document is generally considered
apocryphal. Its voice is now gone with the pieces of her taken.

Cf. *Judges* 19.

I am Sela
who sings against the tribes of them,
a song stoppered up in a fired clay vial.
I sing against the man and men
who would give me up and give me trial.

For shekels my father sold my body
to a brother of a far off land.
For shekels!
But my father did not see

that with my body
went the rest of me.
And with his trade in hand,
my father bowed unto the man.
He bowed!

For all daughters I sing against the tribes of men.

Despite his given shekels, he was tender.
His body, hard and smooth, moved gently,
making warm the bed
and me, without and within
so that I thought, silly girl,
that from love would come love.
But when the storms came,
he brought his asses in
and sent me out.

For body servants I sing against the tribes of men.

And when my womb came alive
I told him so.
To share, to hope, to dream
to see if love could come from love.
It was not so.
He sent me to the stables to be cold,
said if a boy I might return
and if a girl he'd recover his payment,
shekel for shekel.

For all mothers I sing against the tribes of men.

I rose up and stole away,
stole unto my father's house
there to seek an ancient woman
to receive her secret arts.
But when my Master heard of this
he followed on, to claim me home.
My father bowed and feasted him.
For days he bowed and feasted him.
And the while I stole out to the woman
for to work her skills upon me.

For the empty-wombed I mourn and sing against the tribes of men.

We traveled back to my Master's house,
my Master and I, his asses and servant.
We broke the journey through a foreign land,
And were given hospitality.
But the brethren men of that place
came pounding at the door.
Yelling and wanting to know my Master.
He grabbed me by my hair
and tossed me to them, saying,
"Rather do there what you will."
Throughout the night I was bruised and torn
as each came upon me in turn.
With the dawn I crawled upon the doorstep,
and fell into a deathly sleep.

For the preyed upon I sing against the tribes of men.

In my Master's house
I lie beneath him now.

He pushes hard and sweats.
I feel the tear and bruise
that would leave me in shreds.
Above me now he pushes hard and sweats,
a frightful glare in his eye,
a knife between his teeth.
I am lost to him, and all,
impure
not worth a shekel.
Here I lie, lost to him and all,
fearing the thought behind his eye
and the act from out his mouth.

I wail for the lost verses to come.
And to all my sisters, I beg you to sing with me
this song against the tribes of men. (Selah.)

Kimberley
Reynolds

Ode to Elsa

Giver of human meaning
black mass of obedient emotion rarely squirming,
lover of water, shaking like a rivulet as you step
from the pond. Ventriloquist in a side-show circus,
speaking in place of your youngest charge, like a beacon
who knew how to aim our days, children draping you in
glasses and jerseys like a mannequin in a department store.
Babysitter like a blousy Wednesday or Nana in Peter Pan,
some stout-loving Nanny McPhee.
Fragile by my side as a puppy, heeling so close
I nearly kicked you, and truthfully,
I admit, in the haze of postpartum care,
night after night by the crate and the whining,
sticking my hand between the grates,
I wanted to send you back.
But your careful-coated attendance
nursed me back. Juggernaut of love, a naughty aunt

begging for the choicest piece of meat.
Mother to mother I hoarded our daily walks and runs
against the backdrop of a fog-encrusted morning,
snow-dotted black fur and snout
turning gray then white, brown eyes clouded.
And ever in sync with life around you as you lay
on the brown pillow, tail thumping and movement minimal,
like a chew toy frayed at the edges but complete.
We lay with you then, spread out like Cleopatra or
Caesar, reclining on mattresses, distilling your days.
It's not a surprise then that you made the final walk,
your friendship a star aloft.

Lorraine Ryan

Beyond the Garden

Dear Outsiders,

"Even the most beautiful of wildflowers are considered weeds in the wrong gardens."

— Beau Taplin, Wildflowers

It is quiet now.

An easy wind brushes the treetops and high grass but that's the only sound to touch my ears. I have always needed varying degrees of solitude because it's the only time I can truly breathe. Arranging a balance between aloneness and living comfortably with others is never easy for me, but after good fortune and opportunity placed the ideal house in my sights, I thought I finally had mastered the formula. A country home with acres of private fields, two thriving ponds and a small apple orchard fills our souls with a bucolic calm.

And when the blessed peace proves too much for my city-born husband, we're only forty minutes away from the pulse and vibrancy of Boston.

My friends tell me I live a charmed life. Some days I believe it.

Each morning I'm the first one up, leaving Sam softly snoring in the king-sized bed I insisted we buy one week after Maura was born. He didn't understand the need to leave our little nest, our snuggly full-sized bed to something Cirque du Soleil acrobats could happily use for rehearsals. But soon he adapted, as he often does. Our little miracle baby seems to have firmly separated us, like once joined continents. Did becoming parents and the addition of one tiny human cause a marital rift in our bedroom?

Being the only one up is never a lonely thing for me. Padding down the stairs to get the coffee going and not sharing the heady scent of freshly ground coffee beans with anyone is an exquisite start to the day. The morning is all mine, except for Lily, my Russian Blue cat who gently weaves in and out of my legs, a polite reminder that she would appreciate some food. Her silky coat of shimmering gray begs to be fondled and stroked and I take pleasure in knowing that I am the only one she allows to touch her beyond the briefest of moments.

A hawk shrieks outside. Lily freezes and crouches, perhaps remembering a close encounter with this bird of prey.

With a full mug of steaming dark roast to warm my hands, I head for the kitchen nook where I can stretch my legs on chintz window seat cushions that I learned how to upholster from a YouTube video one endless winter. The view from the window never ceases to fill me with wonder and gratitude. Beyond my well-behaved garden of geraniums, asters, violets, irises, and my newly acquired Oriental poppies are the wildflowers, here before my family moved in and probably before generations preceding us. Scattered throughout the field, they live lives full of abandonment, allowing the wind to move them to sensually dance and the sun to have them stretch, stretch toward the sky. Early in the morning I feel a sisterhood—I think of them as female—with these untamed masterpieces and silently promise that I will never confine any flower to a manicured garden where they must neatly stay in rows and do as they're told. Where they are dependent on someone else for their survival, their very life.

The sound of feet hitting the floor upstairs wakes me from my reverie and as always, I must share the morning with the rest of the world, or at least the rest of my family. Maura wakes up grumpy and needs time before she can be addressed. She is beyond her years at six and I often wonder what she will be like in ten years, in twenty years. Although my darling girl fought with a surprising fierceness against leaving the safeness of home for an uncertain school room, she soon accepted and then loved the change. She reminds me of Sam in this way.

Maura stomps her way to the kitchen. I want to tousle her irresistible cornsilk curls but pull back until she finishes her breakfast that I place before her with a cautious smile, like a zookeeper feeding a lion. She announced a few months ago that Irish oatmeal now is the replacement for Froot Loops. She had looked at Sam and me and asked why we let her eat this horrible bowl of sugared poison. We could not come up with a good reason, just as she could not tell us why oatmeal and why it must be Irish.

The clanging of pipes lets me know that Sam is in the shower. I tighten the tie on my robe and start his breakfast. Two eggs over easy, two pieces of lightly toasted wheat bread, orange juice and Earl Grey tea, no milk, one sugar. Always. After everyone leaves the house, I will go for my run and make my kale and blueberry smoothie with almond yogurt, obnoxiously healthy. Always.

I sip my now tepid coffee and watch a wildflower ballet beyond the garden. When had my life become so manicured?

Sam dances his way down the stairs like old-time movie star Fred Astaire and whips into the kitchen. Maura, Lily and I glare at him, but only at first because no one can resist the charms of a happy morning man.

When he runs both hands through Maura's hair and creates staticky havoc, she bubbles up with sweet laughter. Ten minutes earlier she would have screamed at the intimacy. We alternately talk about our plans for the day or lapse into thoughtful silence. Our family has the fit of well-worn slippers; each toe settles in its comfortable place.

Sam drives Maura to school on his way to work, but she comes home on the bus. As they rush out the door, they present their faces to me for a goodbye kiss, but today I feel a compulsion to embrace them with bear hugs. They laugh at my demonstrative show of love, unexpected but happily accepted. I hold the door open and watch them leave, hand in hand, between my shock of roses, peonies and irises that have considerably narrowed the walk-way. Maura runs to the dogwood tree by the wood rain fence, picks up a pink-tinged blossom and sticks it in her hair. They turn around and smile with a final wave and leave me weighted with a composite of joy, sadness and relief.

I close the door and return to my tranquil space where for much of the day no one calls my name.

After house chores, I reluctantly work on a blog I write for a big landscaper in Connecticut. One fingertip touch sends it off with Wi-Fi magic. I type up Sam's list of potential buyers or sellers for his real estate firm, schedule doctor's appointments for all of us and work on Maura's calendar for a month full of dance classes, play dates, library events, piano classes and a young artists program at the museum. Sam tells me I am our family's pendulum, keeping us in motion and on time. What would we be without you, he whispers on those nights our bodies and spirits unite in scheduled coupling.

The morning is satisfyingly constructive, and I debate if I should push that surge of productivity to the afternoon. Multiple freelance deadlines happen this weekend when working is the very last thing I want to do. I decide to reward myself by decadently reading a novel...in the middle of the afternoon!

I sweep away leaves and grass from the Adirondack chairs positioned between the garden and the field, then settle in with a tall glass of iced tea, a huge chocolate-chip cookie, and the *New York Times* best seller I have wanted to read since last Christmas. When I look up, the hawk is still circling the field.

Before I can read the first sentence, Lily stealthily creeps closer, jumps on my lap and with a privilege instinctive to cats, inserts herself between me and the book. I scratch under her chin and croon nonsensical words to her. We enjoy the sun, warm air and quiet together. Maura will be home soon, and a frantic pace will begin when we drive into town for her dance class, then a stop at the farm stand.

The hawk cries and Lily freezes on my lap.

There is a change emerging inside me I can't ignore. Not for the first time I realize my desire, this need for solitary time has grown, stretching beyond the real and imagined borders of family life. Obviously, there is no formula for contentment for me. And I am a fool to trick myself into believing I am the perfect mother and wife. And I am a bigger fool to trick my beautiful family into believing it.

Did pregnancy and sharing my body create an added resentment within me? Perhaps. Sam and I easily lived separate lives for years. We have our different interests and even friends we rarely if ever share. It wasn't until Maura came into our lives that this separation of worlds didn't quite work.

Wanting to be alone much of the time has nothing to do with how much I love Sam or Maura. I try to convince myself of this. And then an embryonic question forms inside me that I can no longer push away.

If I were given the chance to rewrite my life, would I change—I hold my breath, unable to go on. To utter these words, to even think these words is unimaginable. I should stop and not allow any further thoughts to come into my head. Some of my friends opted for divorce and no one seemed unscathed during the ordeal. When Maura was born and placed into my open arms, my heart shattered from unparalleled joy. She is an amazing child whose beauty shines both inside and out and her intelligence and curiosity continue to astound us. My Sam is a perfect companion, an adoring husband, a brilliant entrepreneur and a giving lover. My life seemed to intensify and glow when he entered it. Living in a world without Sam or Maura is unthinkable, wrong.

The hawk flies overhead, screeching, diving, sharp talons out to capture and coldly kill a field mouse, a chipmunk, a cat. I reach out to hold Lily closer. Maura will be home soon. I should get up so I will be there before she gets off the bus. But I don't move.

Leaning back against the chair, I watch carefree lupine, Queen Anne's lace, black-eyed Susans, and phlox sway in the soft wind, each showcasing their unique composition. I close my eyes and free my spirit to roam and cavort among all the wildflowers. A stirring from deep inside me, an explosion of knowing and I understand their singularity, their uniqueness within the field of grass. But as the wind increases, the flowers interlace with the tall grass until they dance together, a sensual ballet, but a tangled choreography that swallows their individuality.

Lily rearranges her body on my lap, knocking the book on the ground. The question, that tantalizing question hangs over my head like a tenacious cloud, dark with threatened possibilities, on a perfect day. I reach up to embrace the unthinkable question, inhaling its depth and breadth and prepare to answer it. If I could rewrite my story and I am saying rewrite my life, drastically changing it, would I? Could I eliminate obstacles in my search for personal freedom? An answer floats around in my mind like in a Magic 8 Ball and when it appears, I am not surprised. And I am prepared.

The rumble of the school bus approaching, phooshes to a stop, the clack of the door opening, and I am at a high alert. Maura will have stepped off the bus and wonder where I am.

I am frozen in the moment. There is a quickening I feel in the air, the earth, and the wind, slight but true. The cat has left my lap and disappeared.

Waiting. Maura often runs into the garden if I am not out front, which is often, I realize. She does not appear. And as a different quiet permeates my new world, I know she never will.

Now and for whatever my forever will be, I have my world to live in as I please. Discovering that early mornings' respites are something entirely different when they extend through the day and tasting the edge of loneliness is bitter, but nothing comes without a cost. My days are spent on the other side of the garden. I alternately thrive with abandoned joy when I run through the tall grass or deteriorate into bottomless sorrow when I gaze at the silent house and up to my daughter's bedroom on the second floor.

On the saddest of days when I look at the house, I remember Sam and his crooked smile and my beautiful daughter with the cornsilk hair. Sometimes I think I can see Maura, now a grown woman. Her lovely face is in profile as she searches the landscape, the fields, the garden in ruins. And always, her face will turn to look beyond the garden and her mournful eyes will find mine.

Wendy
Hoffman

———————

Apparition

Tides wash up strewn splinters
of colored glass and bits of iridescent shell.

I am careful not to cut my foot,
as pangs slice my being in half.

Gulls sip, breezes grand jete, waves shriek.

Memories spill onto this undulating shore,
those I never forgot but did not remember,

tucked between mundane living
and frozen-timelessness,

gentle kindnesses, but words, looks that wrench
my body arching.

I re-meet people and dogs alive to me again
and not corpses that floated away long ago.

Swimming I see bed jackets, potato bakers,
smell the creaminess of pot cheese

and hold all this in my old heart that re-births infancy,
childhood, times of hope, sureness.

My head twists to this enchanted other-land
where waters dance. Sirens, inaudible

voices, lyres, spirits echo.

Ana Burtnett

Winter Trees VII

I remember the winter trees
tucked far into that quiet place.

Beeches playing their tiny castanets,
pines capturing the silver light flowing unchecked over branches
and returning it as the deepest greens,
birches happy enough to be one with the snow.

And that oak felled by a summer storm
its roots pointing so urgently we just had to look up.

These winter trees,
witnesses to our secrets
and caches of ache,

where I visit and every ring is a dream.

Ana Burtnett

Petition to the Goddess of Sleep

We have been true companions for so long
But now when I need you most your visits are brief
You used to be punctual after crisp sheets beckoned to be weighted
You would sing sweet songs and curl yourself around me until the
　　sun lifted us

Lately you've been slipping away while the crickets are still gossiping
I've seen you wandering in the garden drifting between the scarlet
　　runners
And nodding at the blueberries

The other night I caught you peering at the leftovers in the fridge
"Over here!" I whispered
You looked up sheepishly and put down the meatloaf

You took my hand

Folded me back into blankets
Sang sweet songs
And sat in the dim light
Reading *The New Yorker*

Ana Burtnett

Something II

I have dead-headed all the calendula before they got too
    presumptuous
I watered the rhododendron even though they may not make it
Noted which flowers have faded and need to be pulled
Ate toast and homemade jam as the sky turned from orange to blue
Until the holes in heaven reappeared

I hear a voice "Shouldn't you be doing something?"

I didn't find a cure for anything today
Nor did I have an epiphany
I didn't write the President or compose a treatise on an urgent
    matter

I did open the windows to welcome the heady night air
I nurtured the season's hard work

I said good-bye to some of that hard work
I tasted all the sweetness while seeing that the sun has shifted just a
    bit more to the south

Sharon Lopez
Mooney

Pradaxa

I am old
my skin turns
the color of serious sin
at the slightest bump or rub
draws a bruise that earns sympathy
and not quite hidden repulsion from others,
at eighty this leathery hide wears
its history of guts against the norm,
voice a little too loud for their liking
all recorded on skin with onion-paper texture
specially designed with a gazillion lines,
a watershed topical map displaying
the challenge of aging—to learn to live less
with more effort, still against their idea of female,
a weathered elder continuing to embrace
beauty of a different sort,
the crisply wrinkled kind of beauty

as it looks back from the mirror
in morning light

Anne Bower

Simply Chance

How to speak of cancer with eloquence,
with calm resolve, early panic turned mellow?
Realize it's not your fault. It's simply chance.

Stop with the guesswork, that mad mental dance—
If I'd not smoked, not chased that last thrill. No
way thus to speak of cancer with eloquence.

Lucky this time, the cells' wild prance
caught early before crazed rampant billow.
Remember—it's not your fault. It's simply chance.

Surgery's over, stitches sealed by work of lance,
rest now against your own bed's pillow.
Can you still speak of cancer with eloquence?

One day soon your family romance
through normal ups and downs again will flow.

Realize cancer's not your fault. It's simply chance.

I know—once scarred you always cast a backward glance,
fear return, what some damned test will show.
But you've learned to speak of cancer with eloquence,
earned your wisdom—it's simply chance.

Anne Bower

After Reading "I Sit and Sew" by Alice Moore Dunbar-Nelson

This needle with its long tail of thin gray wool
dodges in and out the afghan squares' seams.

The world's too full,
terrors mangling hopes and dreams
with bombs and bullets, lives lost and bloodied,
swaths of forest burned, soil turned foul
despite garnered wisdom, what science
teaches of warfare, climate change,
corporate pillage.

And my needle dodges in and out.

Refugees flee drug wars, tyrants, rising seas.

Poisons fill our rivers, breasts, children,
even seals and seagulls. We've lost so many bees,
so many creatures from tropic to tundra.
We've ravaged the earth for its coal, oil, its trees,
closing our eyes to earth's natural wonder.

And my needle journeys on,
the wool, soft and pale,
fingers working the afghan whole.

Robert Rosen

Original Sin

Just as sin entered the world through one person, and death through sin, death came to all people, because all sinned.

- Paul's Epistle to the Romans, 5:12-21

Captain Orcas B. Wilder stands amongst his 480 ghosts in blue uniforms. They were 1,000 at enlistment, but that was before the Slaughter Pen and Fredericksburg. The Captain's wretched beard sweeps across his waist; his face is hidden under a crumpled Union Kepi cap. He paces out the scrap of land they have to hold, calling out in a thin high voice that struggles against the hot breeze, "Dig for your lives, dig for your lives."

As their sweaty necks chafe red against wool collars under a scorching sun, they try. But the tectonic massif of rock that is Farmer Raffensberger's hill won't yield to their government-issued wood shovels. Jonathan Goodspeed places his shovel on the edge of a two-foot stone and levers it up. He lifts with both hands and waddles to the crest of the ridge as he looks about. When he finds the spot he wants, he drops the stone. He does it a second time and a third, carefully stacking each rock as the others stop to watch, arms crossed over their chests. Now they begin to pry and lift as well. Ordered, placed, fitted, and shimmed, the stones become a fieldstone wall at the crest of what in 24 hours will become Cemetery Ridge.

The captain, always the believer, stands by Jonathan, last in the line on the left. Hand on Jonathan's shoulder, he whispers, "Another regiment is coming to cover your flank."

Looking across the field of grass at the growing grey mob, apparitions shimmering in the heat, Jonathan mutters, "Better get here soon." Believer, skeptic, they've played this out together many times before.

They come from the Mad River Valley, dead center of Vermont. Jonathan took his first steps in those fields; his tiny thumbs pushed seeds into its dark soil. He played with the rusted tin sugaring buckets, crushed on their sides in the cook-fire remains of the Valley ancestors: the Abenaki, the French, and the New Yorkers. He ran his hands over the upthrust rocks and felt their story of the Valley's birth, clawed from the heart of the Green Mountains by a glacier that lost its grip on a warming world.

Second of five, Jonathan would have stayed forever, but there is no such thing as forever. Oldest brother Stephen stood to inherit the 42-acre farm. Jonathan, the second son, knew that he must find his inheritance elsewhere, beyond the Valley. Then the President called for volunteers.

Orcas enlisted first into the Vermont 13th. He was commissioned captain and formed Company B. Jonathan and all the other second and third and fourth sons were recruited with the offer of a way out, a chance for adventure, and a $300 signing bonus with which to begin a fresh start.

The captain always finished his work first in the one-room schoolhouse at the four corners intersection of East Warren and

Roxbury roads. He always helped Jonathan and the other children with their lessons. Always filled the firewood sledge and pulled it to the schoolhouse door on fierce winter mornings. Led them all to Warren Falls on summer Sabbath days where they'd climb the narrow canyon walls. When the captain marked out just the right spot at the cliff's edge, he would jump. They would follow, one by one, falling through uncertain air into the roiling water below.

Jonathan was 15, too young to enlist. His father Saul was at first unwilling to give consent. But the captain promised to look out for the boy and Jonathan was adamant: "I'll be gone soon one way or another." Saul stared at the two for a moment, closed his eyes, and relented. Jonathan's mother and his three younger sisters were a chorus of tears as they said their goodbyes. Saul reached deep into the pocket of his overalls, removed an 1809 Silver Railway Time-keeper pocket watch, and placed it in Jonathan's hand. Jonathan looked down from his father's dead cold stare, ran his thumb over the watch's smooth metal cover, flipped it open, watched the second hand spin while a portrait of his family looked back at him from the inside of the cover, forever gunpowder flash frozen in a daguerreotype photo.

Saul said quietly, "Write us every day you can. Listen to the Captain. It's not your fight. Don't be a hero."

Jonathan nodded. He heard, but he wasn't listening.

Company B trained in the fields, manual of arms, target prac-tice, basic maneuvers. In the fall they mustered with the other companies of the Vermont 13th at Bennington, then headed to Washington, D.C.

On the moonless evening of December 7, 1862, Jonathan stood on duty at a picket station in a grove of tall, dark pines and chest-nut and gum trees that stretched for miles into Maryland. Jonathan thought he saw ghostly shapes moving about in the pitch-black. They could be enemy scouts, or pilgrims grimly marching north.

He sang out, "Halt! Who goes there?"

A voice answered, "Nobody but poor colored folks." A mother holding a small infant and her four girls advanced into the torchlight. The two oldest girls, each with their bundled belongings, led their sisters by the hand.

"Are you cold?" As the words tumbled out of his mouth, Jonathan saw they were all shivering.

"Indeed," the mother replied, "The two smallest are so cold they can't hardly walk. Manda," the mother motioned to the smallest girl, "is beat. So she's lame."

Beat, the word went by without recognition as Jonathan led them into the guard house, made some coffee, fed them bread and pork. By the light of the fire he saw the scars on the mother's face. Her forehead was purple and mashed. The children's faces and noses were skinned and bruised. Jonathan had never seen a slave before. He thought it would be impolite to ask about the wounds, so he chattered on.

"How long have you been coming?"

"Two nights."

"What made you run away?" *Stupid question,* he thought.

"They beat us so. We could not stand it. Twas allus hard, but since the war broke out and my husband lef', they beat us harder than ever."

No one beat anyone in the Mad River Valley, Jonathan thought.

"What is this little one whipped so for?"

"She could not lift a bucket of water. We hid in the pine forest two days before we started. Traveled all night. Then laid over at the house of a colored friend. Next day we started at six and traveled 18 miles till one o'clock. I carried the babe all the way, expecting to be followed by the Master. We pushed hard all night to get to the Union Lines. Can my Master come and get us?"

"No." Jonathan said. Feeling an anger rise inside him, he wagged his head towards the fifteen rifles stacked close by. It was a freezing night, they all slept soundly in the soldier's blankets.

Winter passed, spring came, and the 13th joined First Corps, Army of the Potomac, searching for Robert E. Lee's Army of Virginia. July 1, 1863, the two armies collided at the Gettysburg crossroads, 141 miles west of Philadelphia. In the surprise and confusion that followed, Lee, ever the clear-eyed one, managed to collect his units first and send them, a broad grey arrow, to flank First Corps. The corps, as fearful of Lee's reputation as the reality of the situation, retreated to high ground on Raffensberger's Hill. The corps commander hastily formed them into a rough fish-hook-shaped defensive line with the Vermont 13th in the dead center, and ordered them to dig in.

In the afternoon heat of July 2, the thunder of cannons and the crackle of musket fire roll in from the distance. Company B builds its fieldstone wall. Lee's Confederates test the ends of the Union position at picturesque locations that future tourist park guides will refer to as The Valley of Death and the Devil's Den.

That evening at the campfire, Jonathan takes the pen and stationery he bought off the back of a victualer's wagon and stares at the envelope engraved with a camp scene. He writes his family about the marches. "The food is plentiful and awful. My uniform jacket is too tight. Its bursting buttons and the wool, much coarser than what we spin on the farm, make me look like a circus clown." He looks about for a moment at the rocky soil, which reminds him of home and continues, "In battle, the most fault I find is the unpleasant sound of various dense bodies moving through the air with great velocity." And recounts that "A minie ball cut my hair just above my right ear but did not hurt." He finishes, "Your devoted son, Jonathan," seals the envelope, and writes the words,

"Soldier's Letter" next to the address, so he can mail it at no charge. Without a thought, his hand slides the letter into his right boot.

At 1:00 p.m., July 3, 1863, General Lee orders Major General George Pickett to attack Cemetery Ridge. One hundred fifty Confederate cannons, infuriate demons, come to life, mouths ablaze with tongues of living fire. Their smokey sulphur-laden breath rolls over the ground amongst the artillerymen. These grimy willing ministers frenzy about feeding dusky black globes down smoothbore barrels. They set and ignite fuses, then cover their ears as iron hail is vomited up through the heat of the day. The air is whirring, shrieking, hissing with sounds of solid shot. Bursting shells thunderously split the darkened sky, remote, near, deafening, ear piercing, astounding. Arms, heads, blankets, guns, and knapsacks are tossed into the air and fall back onto the trembling ground around Jonathan.

At 2:30 the sky goes still in a swirling smoke. A bugle calls out the order: "Charge!" The grey mob of apparitions, now 12,300 strong, marches steadily 538 yards across the field towards Raffensberger's Hill—to give everything for nothing. Most don't own slaves. None can lay claim to the sprawling plantations of the lower Mississippi with more millionaires per capita in that moment than anywhere in the world. They march steadily into a new age, with railroads and factories and electricity and ticker tape—none of which will be theirs. In the shade of a peach orchard, British, French, Austro-Hungarian, and Prussian officer cadets picnic in camp chairs taking notes, preparing for the wars of the next century, to be gilded with blood—of their own children.

Jonathan stubbornly grips his Springfield Model 1861 rifled musket, flips up the two leaf sites, shoulders the weapon, and shivers as he leans forward against the south side of his wall, steadying himself on a large boulder. He's thinking of the little girl trying to lift buckets of water as he aims at an officer riding horseback. He barely notices the white feather waving gaily from the man's Hardee hat. At 400 yards, the second hand of his watch deep in his left pocket swings past twelve as Jonathan closes his eyes, pulls the trigger and a black powder cloud erupts. When he opens his eyes, the white feather is gone. Jonathan reaches into his belt, grabs another cartridge, gnaws off the paper wrapper, pours its black powder and musket ball down the barrel, and uses the ramrod and the paper wrapper to tamp the package tight. He flips down the far leaf sight, cocks the hammer, and lets the remaining sight hover on another man, now much closer, waving a Confederate flag. The secondhand of the Railway Timekeeper sweeps past six as Jonathan, this time without a thought, squeezes the trigger again. The flag tumbles to the ground, and just as quickly rises again.

Jonathan hurriedly loads his rifle one final time. They are close, no need to aim. He fires from his hip into the advancing grey blur, reaches around the back of his belt, unhooks an 18-inch steel ring bayonet, slides it over the muzzle of his rifle, and locks it into place just as a tangled wave of arms and legs crest the fieldstone wall. A dam of Union rifles and bayonets holds the wave back at the point of impact, but in a moment of dilated time the wave rolls relentlessly left and pours into the still-uncovered flank just beyond.

Jonathan is pushed forward from behind into the gray mass. Acrid black powder fog chokes his eyes, his nose, his mouth. Something explodes inside him as he becomes a berserker, stabbing his bayonet with a trance-like fury into the swirling blue-grey smoke. The bayonet detaches from his rifle when it embeds in the soft flesh of an advancing soldier. Grabbing the stock of his rifle with both hands he bludgeons a path through the melee, then slips and falls onto a blood-slicked carpet of bodies. Pushing himself to his knees, he can advance no farther as he finds his rifle perpendicularly crossed and locked against the rifle of a grey-jacketed giant who looms over him.

The Confederate soldier and gravity force Jonathan and his rifle back to earth. The Confederate soldier places a knee on Jonathan's rifle as he simultaneously pivots his own rifle and slides his bayonet down towards Jonathan's chest. Jonathan grasps at the blade, but it slides between his hands, pressed against each other as if in prayer. The blade slides through his coat, past his watch, and into the left side of his chest. He feels the cold finger of steel touching things that have never before been touched, ribs, lungs, heart. The second hand of the Silver Railway Timer passes the six, 90 seconds in all, as the Confederate soldier leans in on the butt of his rifle. Jonathan hears the giant's comforting, "Shhh," as he watches his own legs jerk and then relax. He looks with awe into the face of sudden unexpected death. Asks "Why?" as his lungs stop breathing and his heart stops beating. In answer, the center of his temporal lobe suddenly unleashes the collective memories with which we are all born, but willfully forget until the moment we leave this existence. Now, Jonathan's pocket watch begins to spin backward.

A moment of blackness and quiet. Then Jonathan feels the ribs of a boat pushing into his back. A voice sternly barks, "Quit lying down, up on your feet soldier!" Jonathan obeys and re-beholds the stars. An angel boat person stands in front of him on the thwarts of the small skiff. She seems almost massless, and yet with each stroke of her long oar the boat surges toward the Pillars of Hercules. Behind rises a mountain, unlike any he's ever seen before. It's like some topsy-turvy circular layer cake floating on a shimmering sea. A road runs on its surface, spiraling upward, pulsing alive with a moving mass of pilgrims marching along until they disappear into a copse of woods covering the peak.

The skiff slides up on the beach. The voice commands, "Prepare to march."

Jonathan tentatively takes a few steps on a path before him. He wonders if each is purposeful, or in vain. He's driven by a desire to leave worldly sorrow and misery and enter a state of grace. Somehow he knows that can only happen when sin is absolved.

A circle of air shimmers just more than a man's height above the beach. A neon sign below flashes *Hammurabi, sixth king of Babylon,* in cheesy green script. Jonathan stops and curiously looks inside to see the long braids of Hammurabi's beard stubbornly refuse to obey either laws or authority as they slide across his father's chest. Hammurabi greedily works the signet ring off the swollen finger of his dying father's hand and places it upon his own ring finger, crowning himself king. A scribe sits nearby at a table lit by a small brass lamp.

The King says, "Tell them now that I am now the Law Giver."

The scribe lifts a wedge-tipped reed stylus and presses cuneiform shapes into a tablet. "The people whose mountains are distant and whose languages are obscure, I will put straight their confused minds with a Code of Laws."

The king rises and walks into a courtyard dominated by a seven-foot-tall basalt stele he's greedily plundered from a neighboring kingdom. "My gift to the people," he says, broadly waving a hand.

The scribe picks up his tablet and hurries behind, smirking as he remembers the King a as saying, "My gift to the people, to prevent the strong from oppressing the weak."

The king stares at the cramped inscriptions that loop the polished black object. They say nothing to him, for he cannot read. "Where do we start tonight?"

"Sixteenth law." The scribe's eyes stare at the ground.

"Laws for the conquered peoples then."

"Slaves," the scribe writes the word, for the first time ever.

The king, impotent in the extended silence, roars, "Read it to me!"

"If anyone receives into his house a runaway slave and does not bring it out at the public proclamation of the major domus, they shall be put to death."

"And a reward?"

The scribe pauses. The king, misreading indecision for insolence, scowls. The reed moves again, writing the new law. "If anyone find runaway slaves in open country and bring them to their masters, the master shall pay him five shekels of silver."

"Two shekels."

The scribe presses thumb to soft clay, obliterates the five, and replaces it with a two-stroke symbol, setting the first price on a human being.

Hammurabi suddenly notices a dark spot floating in the middle of the room. In the reflected light he sees Jonathan's face, observing one answer to his question without expression. The event horizon of Purgatory pulls Hammurabi gently into the dark spot. He does not resist. A bronze battle cuirass over a white robe falls through the air, two heavy leather sandals land upon the beach, and Jonathan casually says, "The price of a slave is now three-fifths a free person," and wags his head in the direction he is headed. Hammurabi falls in and the two resume the march up the path towards dawn. The shadow of the towering mountain covers much of the horizon line. Dark clouds hang just below the peak, obscuring the midsection as they flicker to the crackle of static.

Jonathan Goodspeed's executioner appears ahead in another shimmering circle of air. He's never killed another person before. Awkwardly, he neatens the body, placing Jonathan's corporeal hands across his chest. He picks up his own rifle and moves on, taking care as he steps over Jonathan's blood-mocked uniform. Then he stops, sobs, and steps through the portal, his head searching for comfort on Jonathan's shoulder. For a moment Jonathan feels alive again as he hugs the soldier tightly in a forgiving embrace.

Just beyond, a herd of goats and ibex mingle on a rocky outcropping, uninterested as the three men march by, circling the mountain. On the mountainsides, moving museum dioramas show Persian King Cyrus the Great's war chariot rolling down the boulevards of a conquered Babylon, pulled by Hammurabi's defeated soldiers, now slaves under the lash. Greek King Alexander the Great's diamond of cavalrymen cut through successive serried ranks of the same slave soldiers as Persian Emperor Darius III wheels his chariot in retreat. Roman praetor Servius Sulpicius Galba toasts his warrior guests seated at long tables in a Lusitanian meadow. Fire arrows arc through the sky as Roman archers hidden in the woods ambush the guests, then lead the survivors into the mines of Rio Tinto to spend 1,000 years digging Roman silver before they emerge as the Portuguese. The crowd of pilgrims grows behind Jonathan as the players, scene by scene, all step out on the path to join the march to the summit.

On the other side of the mountain, the sun shines harshly upon a whitewashed fortress perched atop a cliff overlooking a beach. Portuguese Prince Henry the Navigator stands at a rampart holding his expansive black chaperon in place against the stiff sea breeze. Across the bay, a light-footed merchant ship beats smartly into the wind. Antam Gonçalves, wiry, face not yet full of beard, stands on the stern deck directing the crew to reset the lateen sails. They leave the white-capped ocean and enter the harbor, completing their voyage prowling West Africa. Below deck they hold a dozen kidnapped African men and women in chains.

The Prince joyously mutters to the small man with a long face standing next to him, "It's not so much for the number of captives taken, but for prospect of the countless other captives that will be taken." The small man pulls his gold embroidered papal cape more tightly about his shoulders against the breeze. His hawk-like nose protrudes from under a tall conical papal hat. He imagines the kidnapped victims held in the hold not as poor innocent souls, but as a few of the heathen bastards that have just captured Constantinople. He turns to his scribe and dictates a Papal decree that grants Portugal the right ". . . to invade, search out, capture, vanquish, and subdue all Saracens and pagans whatsoever …[and] to reduce their persons to perpetual slavery. . ." so long as they are converted to Christianity. When they notice the sea of faces watching from the other side of the portal, the two royals take off their hats and robes and step out into the grey crowd that now follows Jonathan on the path up the mountain.

A cave appears around the next bend; a neon sign hums and crackles as its looping red lines shout out *The Seed of American Slavery*. Jonathan enters the claustrophobic space, sits in a simple folding chair as the small screen at the front lights up.

Illegitimate John Jope, indentured to work off his family's debt, is face down at the local alehouse. His slobbering lips mouth out the words, "Say bummers will you meet us and help revive my soul. I am on my way to Zion, the new Jerusalem." It's a Scottish tune destined to become *The Battle Hymn of the Republic.* Sir Walter Raleigh's press gang enters. They flip the bartender a coin and with wicked smiles lift the listless man from his place and snatch him away for service.

Jope becomes a privateer and is rewarded by Queen Elizabeth with an obsolete warship, the *White Lion,* and a commission. Now it's 1619 and the *White Lion* rocks gently at berth in the fetid August air of Point Comfort, Virginia. Captain Jope hums "Glory, Glory, Hallelujah" as he peers through an iron grate into the dark hold of his rotting ship and counts 20 starving Ndongolese slaves captured from a Portuguese slaver. He and his crew are starving too, so he doesn't bargain when he sells his prize to the Governor of Virginia. Time now loops back on itself, for in the same moment he's planting the seed of slavery in America, Raffensberger's Hill becomes Cemetery Ridge, smeared with human carnage as the battle desperately continues. A blue blur, the promised reinforcements belatedly led by Captain Wilder arrive. The shock of their impact pushes the grey-jacketed soldiers back up over the wall, sweeping away the high-water mark of the Confederacy.

Jonathan is filled with tears as the captain kneels before his own lifeless corporeal body. The captain now looks up apprehensively out of the screen at Jonathan for a sign. Jonathan sadly shakes his head no and whispers, "Save me."

The captain reaches into the right boot of the corpse, retrieves the letter and the pocket watch, second hand still spinning backward. Now the captain stands atop the ridge, war at his feet, blood metallic in his nostrils. For a moment a vision appears, a line of shackled humans of all shapes and sizes and colors stretched across the field. Some are dressed in strange clothes. Some are naked.

One man had a chance to save the ghosts, and the Pilgrims, and the captain, and Jonathan, and the 51,000 who die between July 1 and July 3, 1863. In the summer of 1776 Thomas Jefferson scratches the words, "Life, Liberty, and the Pursuit of Happiness, Inalienable rights" on a sheet of paper. From his desk in a one-room Philadelphia apartment, Jefferson motions to his slave Robert Hemmings to hold the candle closer as he writes in early drafts of the Declaration of Independence that the slave trade is "an execrable commerce" and a "cruel war against human nature itself." But later he removes those words, part of the bargain that begins this country with the other slaveholding Founding Fathers.

Jefferson turns to Jonathan as he passes and beseeches, "I really had no choice." His eyes search for a hint of empathy as Jonathan stands expressionlessly silent in his bloody, mud-caked uniform. Jefferson sighs, steps out on the path, and joins the Pilgrims.

Almost at the top now, Jonathan watches as the captain and the men of the Vermont 13th take care not to let their brothers in arms rot by the fieldstone wall. They cannot wash the blood from their uniforms, so they wrap the dead in their government-issued blankets and bury them, taking care to leave named markers.

They all fear anonymous death, for there are no government-issued dog tags. The soldiers have taken to writing their names on scraps of paper, pinning them to their clothing or carving their names on pieces of wood worn on strings around their necks. Half the dead are listed as simply unknown, but they all now have a place in the crowd of pilgrims that heads up the mountainside.

When no letters arrive for several months and there is no notice from the Army, the Goodspeeds hire one J.S. Foof to investigate. Foof reaches Gettysburg four months after the battle. He writes to the Goodspeeds: "I looked until so dark I could not see to read the names on markers and returned to the hotel a little disappointed."

Foof searches a log barn where he has been told Jonathan is buried. All about, teams of men remove unidentified bodies, taking them to the Soldiers National Cemetery being constructed nearby. Back at his hotel, Foof encounters Miriam Warren, who wrote the Goodspeeds that she believed she knew where the body was buried. Foof and Warren search together for hours, but to no avail. Foof pronounces himself "quite discouraged."

"Jonathan's board is since gone," Foof writes, "either by the cattle in the field, the cemetery trams driving through or by soldiers finding his board down and using it to mark other graves."

Foof doesn't know that Jonathan's body has already been re-covered by the captain and transported north. The captain returns to the Mad River Valley still wishing to fulfill some part of his promise. He stands before Jonathan's brother Stephen, returns the watch and the letter retrieved from Jonathan's boot. Stephen takes the letter and reads the postscript. "I feel that this fever of war is about to peak. When it breaks and my adventure ends, I will gladly return home, just don't make me dig up any more of those damn rocks." Stephen hands the watch back to the captain, thinking *He can sit with it.* They never speak again, fair enough punishment for the captain's sins.

On the road ahead, Jonathan sees the end. Millions of Pilgrims stand in front of a towering gate shut tight. Behind, millions more form a line that includes their group and others, past, present, and future. Jonathan watches as the Goodspeeds bury his body in a small graveyard on the East Warren road, 2,000 feet above the valley below. He can now look west toward the spine of the Green Mountains. He always looked in that direction when he wondered about his future. Jonathan thinks to himself, *when it does arrive and there are no more pilgrims left to wait for, the gate will open, and we will all be set free.*

Mary Schanuel

Life Bends Down to Kiss Life

Near the curve in the road I stop
stunned
by a sudden familiarity.

How could I be here so soon
when I was so confident
I would never get here at all?

Leaning into the breeze
I ponder — needlessly, pointlessly —
when this thing I'm telling you happens:

Life bends down to embrace me,
kissing itself and whispering

"Good job, my love.

You did the best you knew how.
Let go. Be forgiven."

I drink in the chantilly-colored light
and gather my bones
for the short jog ahead.

Tricia Knoll

Of Physics and Milkweed Seed

Glory be to gravity.
I am held.
Whales stay in oceans.
A baby floats, grows
    and moves down to birth.
The cairn grounds the path
    unheeded until I'm lost.

The stacks I build
    of books and bills
    haiku notebooks
fixed, safe and firm.
Valor in not running away
from unanswerable letters.

A scribbled list

of what holds me pendulous–
stout boots, sober and serious
gravitas of loneliness and war
loss and aging. Yet I try

to defy these heavy weights
with banner-waving protest,
private love and poetic justice.
Pearl fog rises, holds tight
to a river valley, misted lid.

My spool loosens
string to the dragon kite.
A tug, a lurch. Ripple-dance
of tethered hand, wind, wing
and lift. Airborne.

Bill
Pendergraft

Mourning Dove

who calls from the emergent pine
across the tidal slough
I, hands cupped my thumbs together, respond
low lonely call of hope
and he calls back, flies closer
here I am at the end of my time
and he alone, searching for others of his kind
I call again and he responds
flies to the laurel thicket
carried by our chorus
so we both perch, call, wait
calling for comfort
calling for mate

in these times
we become both the caller and called

for if we no longer sing
what becomes of us all

Michelle
Cacho-Negrete

That Coldest Winter

That coldest winter we had twenty-two days below zero and it almost never went above freezing. The air outside was a crystal dome I carefully navigated, certain it would shatter in slivers of kaleidoscopic brilliance. My breath was something alien, a lifeform of translucent mist. Snow kept falling that coldest winter, great trembling quilts that shrouded trees, constructed bridges between boulders and tree stumps, obliterated trails, walled in windows and doors leaving our house gloomy and dark until Kevin shoveled to let light in and us out. The house we owned was at the end of a nearly deserted road that the snowplows reached days after a snowfall as if it were an afterthought. We were surrounded on three sides by a forest and thick bandages of snow bound trees together. We heated with a woodstove that resembled the glowing red of an all-seeing eye. Cords of wood stacked in a woodshed were a wall of fungus-coated logs. If we slept through a whole night without waking to feed it, the air grew so dense with cold it seemed impenetrable. As that coldest winter continued, our house became a battleground, cold the victor until we'd coaxed kindling, old newspaper, dry wood into a flaming roar of victory.

I had too often been alone in winter, huddled in front of the woodstove praying for the melancholy song of the plows. I'd pull on snowshoes and wander the forest wishing for a prince to rescue me. That coldest winter Kevin was unable to travel for work as he always did. Each day, he'd snow-blow the driveway, inspiring a blizzard of flakes that dressed him in a frosty coat. I was glad he was there and hoped he too would experience feeling trapped in this frozen world. We were different people, however, and he vanished nearly the whole day to his attic office to work or read while I wrote downstairs, then snowshoed longing for city streets.

"Don't you love solitude?" he asked.

"Not for weeks at a time," I answered.

After the snowplows departed, their hieroglyphics of tire tracks identifying the white, pebble-strewn road, we hurried out to the grocery store, walked in the nearby town, browsed the secondhand bookstore. The road back home was a wall of white streaked with black exhaust we peeked around like timid animals before each turn and stop sign. We couldn't outrun the night no matter what time we drove back. It always hovered, prepared to engulf us. It swallowed the nine miles of road home, our headlights ripping only the narrowest path through the blackness.

We argued about moving as we hauled in firewood, the cords diminishing as though some ravenous being swallowed them whole. Kevin was content to gaze at the lichen-covered bark, bring some upstairs to his office microscope, take a nap. I, however, was certain we'd run out of food or firewood, that the road would be impassable, that we wouldn't get out before spring. I also felt uncertain of whether spring's tremulous corridor to summer would be defeated by an unending winter which I felt had defeated my marriage. Kevin, described by co-workers as a self-contained unit, was content with work and books and solitude, but I needed streets and libraries and other people.

The temperature dropped to polar levels. The world metamorphosed each night while we slept; distances lengthened, things shape-shifted, the cold a cocoon with no promise of what would emerge. I was frightened of things I couldn't name, of an unknown menace given free rein to wreak havoc. One morning my car, a hulking metal creature in the barn we used as a garage, refused to start. We hooked cables to Kevin's car battery. I went inside and stared through the frosted window, resigned to being held prisoner. Kevin gave me a thumbs-up when the car hummed its wake-up. I believed it was bound for obsolescence.

The next morning our electricity was dead. The light in the house turned silty gray, radio and television dead, woodstove a glowing beast on which we made coffee and toast, then lentil soup and steamed greens for dinner. We shut down the pipes to prevent freezing. We snowshoed to warm up. We melted snow on the stove to cook, clean dishes, brush our teeth, wash ourselves, flush the toilets. The light through the frost-blinded windows was too dim to read by at three o'clock. Our flashlights were miner's helmets illuminating the darkened room on our way to bed.

I lasted three nights. When the sun rose on the fourth morning, light without warmth to pierce the ice on our bedroom windows, I packed an overnight bag and Kevin, after a few moments of protest, did the same. We drove to the next state, a one-hour drive expanded to three hours, a roller-coaster ride of icy snow ridges. We dragged fallen trees off the road. We passed discarded cars conquered by the deep-frozen air. We passed sad, dark houses, reminders of how helpless humans were against an undefeatable adversary.

At the hotel there were other refugees, women and men, faces wind-burned and sooty-eyed whose children chased each other noisily, excited to sleep in a room with a television and their parents. I drank coffee and ate donuts, an exotic treat. The manager handed out tickets for free drinks at happy hour that night. In our room, I sank into the bathtub, water as hot as possible, my skin red and steaming like I'd been boiled. That night I had two glasses of wine. Everyone in the dining room, temporary companions, exchanged survival stories about falling on ice, cars sliding uncontrollably, getting lost in the darkness.

We stocked up on groceries, went to a restaurant, and saw a film. I felt reborn, then not, as we backtracked home, the exhaust from our car a white contrail in the darkness. The next morning the electricity was back. That morning brought a bit of warmth and a bit of sun that brushed aside the clouds. A day above freezing tentatively arrived, then three, then nearly a week. The cold was reluctant to surrender, a blistery wind invading every corner, but spring was more determined. The days became longer, the sun more aggressive. The snow melted into ice, imbricated layers of treachery shimmering in the sun. Town streets were shields of black ice, thin and transparent, dangerous in their invisibility.

The sun was higher, warmer, claimed more hours. Beneath the ice the desire for escape whispered: crackling, hissing, struggling to escape. One morning we woke to the sound of running water, like a carelessly forgotten faucet, all around us. The snow and ice that had resisted evolution to liquid had given in. A small river encircled our house, forced its way into the basement, swallowed the yard, the front steps, the driveway. The path between our house and barn was obliterated. We pulled on boots and went out to look at the cars. The water barely covered the tire rims and it felt as though they were safe.

That night it dropped to below freezing again, and on the way to our mailbox, I slid on black ice and fell on my left side. Firecrackers exploded through my thumb, wrist, arm as I sprawled beside the mailbox, dazed by the intense pain. I needed the ER. Kevin had heard the impact, at the window, then slipped on shoes and cleats and came to get me. We drove carefully to avoid standing water that could strand us in deep holes. Kevin kept looking over at me, mumbling, "I'm sorry you're hurt," then later said, "You knew there was black ice. You should have worn your cleats."

I barely heard him— I had shifted into an other-world of pain and imagined throwing myself into a pocket of snow to be anesthetized.

The hospital waiting room overflowed; people cushioning arms, legs, elbows, backs, heads. We greeted each other in painful camaraderie, our words those of wounded soldiers describing our injuries and acknowledging defeat by an insidious victor. The doctor read my x-rays, pointed out fractures like sidewalk cracks, administered a numbing pain killer, cast my thumb and wrist, gave us written orders, sent us out into the thawing world. It was late, dark, my fall a seemingly long-ago event. The sky was a deep indigo, fading edges of gold piercing bits of ice that remained on treetops and sequined the road. Town lights faded behind us like an echo until we were enveloped by blackness.

"I'm not going to spend another winter in the house," I said softly.

Kevin was silent, concentrating on the road, then nodded. "OK."

By summer, we had a probable buyer and a house on the outskirts of town. The last carton was packed, last trips to Goodwill made, last housecleaning for whoever finally moved in finished. Kevin had gone on ahead. In the summer heat, crows circled, ready to claim our three acres, the bones of the land released from its frigid prison now seeming infinite. I'd forgotten that coldest winter how much we had: the verdant blueberry bushes where I pulled off handfuls and ate them for the last time. The ancient granite boulders our grandchildren now in college had climbed. The snowshoe path we'd kept immaculate, now green with hungry weeds. A wave of regret almost drowned me, but then, summer is our shortest season. I didn't know if we'd have another winter like the coldest one, but I knew there would be many more to come and I couldn't be here.

I climbed into my car and drove away.

John Sanborn

Pronouns

they sat in the corner,
backs against the wall,
cradling each other,
so small against the confusion
around them in the ER;

traveling here
hoping against age and time
that something could
reclaim anything in
the time left.

he,
        wrapping his arm around
        her slender shoulder,
offering as
much protection as did
the knights of old,

those gallant men who
fought off dragons and
rode into the sunset
with their lady.

she,
    reclining her head
    on his shoulder, and
    tucking into her husband
    like a little chick under
    a mother hen's wing,
closes her eyes
to the inevitable,
    even
    as her mind tries
    to rally with
    expectations of life.

he,
    with his right hand
    resting on his cheek in
    thought and memory,
    and his left arm
     cradling the
    one he loves,
holding the world at bay
and seeking more time
together.

love only takes you so far
and then you have to walk alone.

but that time had not come yet,
the journey together still alive.

Roger Watters

Faces Like Mine

As I enter the auditorium
for the funeral, I see familiar
faces that have aged.
Why are there just
a few faces like
mine looking back?
They are trying to figure
out who I am, just like I am
attempting to do with them.
Smiles evolve when that
feat is accomplished
to a wave of the hand.
The current status of
all in attendance has
been uniquely updated.

Audrey Stibbe

What Is the Definition of the Word "Word"?

Random letters put together
To form a meaning or sound.
How very very profound.
Sarcastic, Bombastic
And even Elastic.
Words that flow off the tongue
Ice Cream you scream we all scream for Ice Cream.
Words that hurt
Words that heal
Words that seem unreal.
Jabberwocky, Mumbo Jumbo
Bibbity Bobbity Boo
And the Owl cried out Whoo Whoo
Words that calm
Words that excite
Words that give you a fright.

Terrify, Petrify
Gruesome,
winsome and lose some

Words of love
Words of kindness
Words that give you a shove.
Bump, Butt, Bulldozer
I called over
You came running
Handed me a note
Filled with words.

Julia Whinston

My Father's Brother

I have only two memories of seeing my uncle in person. My father introduced him to my twin sister and me as "your uncle Alan," well before we knew what the word "uncle" meant. We were three years old at the time. As far as we were concerned, he could have been an old friend, a brother, or even a complete stranger, because that's what he was to us at the time. A strange man who won our love on the unsanded, old wooden porch, producing two beautiful princess dresses he had bought for us to wear. My childhood dog was there, a golden retriever named Sydney (after the 2000 Olympics). She stared at him, mouth agape, tongue hanging, brown eyes wide with fascination. My dress was wispy and violently pink, with a gold and purple petticoat. The soft, cold January breeze blew my sister's soft pink outfit, frosty with white trim around the sleeves and skirt. According to my father years later, my uncle stayed with us for over a month, but the only memory I have of that time was watching *Real Time With Bill Maher,* the stiff couch we'd snuggled on patterned in the 1980s style of its origin, zigzags and stripes like a one-of-a-kind south-western style Kitsch painting.

He never visited again. He disliked traveling to the United States, which only added to his enigmatic allure. My uncle's far-off life seemed like a fairytale to me. A garden backyard within a stone duplex where he lived in Baka Jerusalem. He once described to me, in an email, the hummingbirds that resided in his courtyard pear tree. Every morning, they flew from their nests, little empty slippers, to inspect the morning glories that snaked up the telephone poles. Somewhere far away, at his small kitchen table, he ate toast with butter and orange marmalade, and thought of me because orange was my favorite color. Ours was a bond not of proximity, but of profundity.

Eventually, we put pen to paper and established the exclusive "The Real Letter Club." Together, we penned into existence our sacred rituals, worshiping postcards and stationery, fountain pens and stamps. He sent me poems he had written, stories of Jewish triumph, language riddles to decipher as I learned more Hebrew in Sunday school. He was the biggest fan of my early work (an embarrassing poem about Glacier National Park and an Ode to Tolkien's Smaug, among others). My uncle observed in my words the acuity of early adolescence. He respected what others may have laughed at. Once a year, I would talk to him on the phone, when he called to wish my father a happy birthday. His voice contained within it an eclectic mix of New England and Jerusalem.

When I was thirteen years old, my Uncle Alan gave me a vital piece of advice. "For sadness there is only one cure: ice cream," he wrote to me in an email. My pet turtle had just died, my most formative experience with true grief. The death of my turtle was the first instance of a deep reciprocal relationship ending suddenly in death. I had taken care of my turtle: cleaned its tank, fed it turtle food from the pet store, given it islands to sunbathe on and logs to hide under. In return, my turtle had given me companionship, the feeling of not being alone, having someone to take care of who would give me love and loyalty in return.

"My advice. Go right out, buy another turtle, call it by the same name, and it will be like your turtle has been reborn," my uncle joked. Somehow, this sequence of words transported him. He was ever present, comforting me from thousands of miles away.

Even now, almost ten years later, the email I had sent him makes me emotional. "Dear Uncle Alan," I wrote, "I was just writing because my turtle died and I am really sad and I don't know what to do. Much love, Julia". I can remember feeling despondent, and overwhelmingly like I didn't know what to do with all of the sadness I felt. It seemed too vast to me to be overcome. It was much the same sensation I felt when, later that year, he passed away, too.

I had prepared to beg, plead, and scream for my chance to attend my uncle's funeral, but, as it turned out, I didn't have to. Our family quickly decided that my father and I should go to Israel for the funeral. I was going, and that was that.

When we arrived in Jerusalem to sit Shiva, everyone who came by seemed to know who I was. My uncle had told all of his friends about me, people he often passed on the street on his way to the market. My aunt, his wife, read psalms for each letter of his name, and we prepared ourselves, slowly, in our grief, to travel to his funeral in the town of Rosh Pina. The village was typically romantic and quaint, with red-roofed buildings stacked together and sloping slowly uphill. Old stone promenade-style houses were shoved haphazardly in crevices facing the flat land beyond. Balloons and string lights lined some of the small paved roads. The town was reminiscent of a small Italian village, but still in place with most of Israel in its own exotic, peaceful and dated way. My aunt complained of a recently constructed McDonald's erected at the entry road, out of place amongst its picturesque surroundings. Next to the fast food restaurant was a grove of olive trees, from which wafted the deep timbre of a clarinet. Goats grazed lazily along the fences that lined the sloping, narrow concrete road, most of them white, but a few brown, tan, and black colored goats were scattered among their herd.

Against Jewish custom, my uncle Alan had chosen to be cremated. We buried his ashes between the roots of an old and gnarled tree behind the village. Friends, family, and acquaintances gathered from many different places, their collective cacophonous murmurs echoing in many different languages. In my turn, I had decided to write one last Real Letter Club letter to read to him there. I had worked so hard on it, poured my heart and soul into this one note, but in the end, hardly anyone could understand what I was saying. What I read was through hysterical sobs, strange words I had trouble pronouncing through my tears. I cried as I stood in the dirt of Rosh Pina, smokey, burning sage assaulting my nostrils, alone at the center of a circle of strangers.

I think that everyone understood how much he had meant to me, though. For once, where my uncle was concerned, words had failed me, but my feelings were understood wholly by the collective. My aunt wrote to me after, "I was always so happy to witness this rare relationship that you both had and how you were both so committed to it."

That night, we celebrated Shabbat with my uncle's best friend, a goat farmer who lived there in the village of Rosh Pina. My uncle was dead, but his death had brought me here, closer to my family, to these people who had filled his life with joy. I was elated to be part of it all, to feel like I was starting to get to know the person he was when he wasn't on the computer. I felt him there in that small room as a boy lit the candles and they sang to me. I felt him when I felt God at the Wailing Wall, when I ate a giant Arab bagel in the old city, in an empty alleyway with only one table lining the sidewalk, the area filled with a myriad of exotic smells, and in the scintillating sunlight that shone upon the Dome on the Rock.

That is how I will always remember the holy land. Not for the lack of humanity that defines the word "Israel." Not for war and violence and atrocity. But of that temporary moment of peace, of people grieving side by side. Of clarinet music, children with large kippahs like saucers perched on their small heads, and goats. I acknowledge that for many millions, the privilege to see things this way is inaccessible and remote. It may seem naive and out of touch to many who have resided closer in proximity to such horror. I know that the pain that is still being caused is insurmountable and impossible to quantify. I wanted to write this to remind us—on this side of the ocean—who are confused and angry and passionate, of something that connects us rather than divides us. We can come together and allow grief to beget peace. We are all humans, regardless of those who view us as pawns to sacrifice for power. We can stand up and stand strong together in our grief. Our grief can move mountains.

My uncle wrote to me once, "Is the conflict between Arab and Jew really built on discrimination, the inability to recognize and accept one another as full human beings? I don't know. Human beings are creatures of habit. It seems to be a human habit to discriminate against anything or anyone that is different. I think it is fear. We are afraid of what is different." But in grief and love, we are all the same. We cannot forget that.

Dennis Gray

self therapy

I had to do something
my therapist was showing up
for house calls at dinnertime
after eating a full meal
he said "we went over our hour
but we are finally making progress"
he handed me a bill and said
"have a nice evening"
got in his Karmann Ghia
and drove away

whose therapist drives a Karmann Ghia
I knew it was time to move on
I am making progress

it was costly at first
I had no idea what
I would have to pay for a Ghia

old cars need repairs every day
so I set it up on blocks
in the garage
and just used it for my office
that way my therapy time
would not affect my living

first I suggested I'd take up drinking
we decided black tea over green
and it was important to stop before nine
so I could sleep at night
I didn't understand that right away
since it was my insomnia that started this
I told myself it was important
to write down any changes good or bad
which began to make sense
why didn't he tell me any of this

I started writing things down
but it had nothing to do with tea
there were memories of times in the park
movie theatres and pizza joints
there were faces I hadn't seen in years
and everyone was happy
I wrote about birds and squirrels and flowers
but mostly young ladies that moved me
I remember I never told them
how they made me feel
I couldn't step up because I couldn't decide
I was afraid to close my eyes

I closed my eyes that night

when I woke up I didn't remember a thing
the young ladies were gone
there was melancholy
I could smell old Volkswagen
car oil cigarettes and White Castles
I thought there'd be perfume
lipstick stains and hairspray
I checked my notes
I didn't remember their names
I didn't give myself a chance at heartbreak
because I didn't love

I had the upholstery redone that week

David A.
Hinkhouse

Roadblock

Hunger sets in and concentration slips away.
I couldn't see it coming so I moved ahead.

I had the path well-planned for escape--
middle of the night thunder storm outside,

even better, a little extra help,
no one to owe, just my shadow

which right now feels heavy to drag along,
like a tune I can't get out of my head

that suffocates the songs I like better,
or the cry from a wounded comrade

that freezes me in my tracks at the edge
of quicksand when instinct tells me to run,

or my anguish at having made a friend
in a place where to run makes perfect sense,

or hate aimed at my head like a bullet
or a bullet aimed at my head like hate

or my own fate I do not want to feel
aimed at nothing, aimed at my shadow now

taunting me in the middle of this jungle path,
the roadblock ahead shadowed by my own shadow

as it blunders into enemy territory just ahead of me
as I try to disconnect it from the soles of my feet.

Cynthia
Shepard

Own the Night

Come,
let's forth,
to own the night!

Slip from sheets
in noiseless flight.
Prance 'neath stars
in pure delight!
Unwind knots
that bind us tight.

Immerse ourselves
in cricket song,
A symphony
played summer long.
Dance among the fireflies,
daisies brush against our thighs.

Owl takes to silent wing,
shadows shift near rustling.
Hairs on necks begin to rise…
shivers run straight down our spines!

Come,
let's forth,
to own the night!
Venture out—
make it thine!

Robert Perron

A Push in the Dark

Despite a lack of evidence, every drop of Dan's lifeblood told him his wife's "meetings" had more to do with dalliance than meditation. The way Shannon looked forward to Wednesday night. The way she showered and brushed her hair. Her light goodbye kiss with the promise of a newer, better her upon return. Dan flicked off the television. He wasn't a man of action, but too many Wednesdays had gone by with his stomach in turmoil, and he knew the supposed location of the supposed meeting—a church on Fifth. He rose from the couch and crossed the living room into the hallway of their two-bedroom co-op on the Lower East Side. They both worked for the city transit department, Dan in asset management, Shannon in IT. That's where they met some sixteen years ago.

Dan halted in front of his stepson's door. A second rap elicited a shout from within: "Permission to enter." Ha, ha, his son the comedian. Dan turned the doorknob.

Ryan lay on his oversized twin, head propped by two pillows, thumbs working an 8.7-inch tablet, which provided the only light in the room. Dan sniffed the gray air. But kids did other stuff these days, stuff that didn't have to be lit. At eighteen, Ryan was six foot one, another factoid that gnawed at Dan, those three inches of height the boy had on his stepfather. Not to mention a flat stomach, 20/20 vision, and a full head of hair. He wore his rainbow motif "Gay Lives Matter" T-shirt. A month ago, ignoring Shannon's advice, Dan had broached orientation at the breakfast table. "Dad," Ryan had said. "Are you *against* gay rights?" "Of course not." "Then you're *for* gay rights?" Dan had nodded in acquiescence to the boy's logic. Ryan had leaned toward Dan. "So, does that mean you're gay, because you're for it? And by the way, do you hear *me* asking *you* about your sex life?"

A difficult age for all. Dan pushed on the bridge of his tortoise-shell glasses and stated his business. "I'm going out for a while."

Ryan looked over the top of his tablet. "Cool. Where to?"

"Just going for a walk."

"Is Mom at her feel-good meeting?"

Dan nodded.

"So that makes me master of the apartment."

"Temporarily."

As Dan reached for the doorknob, Ryan said, "Hey, Dad, have you read *Othello*?"

Dan tugged on his right earlobe. "Sure. It's been a while."

"Did you dig it?"

"There wasn't much to dig. Iago got inside Othello's head—"

"I mean, it seems extreme. There's no real proof, and even if there was, you don't just off your spouse for fooling around."

"Yeah, well, I think it's more about Iago. You know, the way he—"

"Then why's it called *Othello*? If you ask me, that guy was whacked."

"Which one?"

"Othello."

"Yeah, well. Is this a school assignment?"

"No, Dad, I just thought I'd torture my brain with Early Modern English."

"I thought they did *Merchant of Venice* and *Julius Caesar*."

"They did." Ryan deepened his voice. "This is the advanced stuff."

"Yeah, well—" Dan sniffed the air and closed his son's door. His son since age two by dint of a predecessor's emission. No additional children for practical reasons. But Dan had developed a love for his quasi-offspring, not only abiding but defending his quirky behavior, taking umbrage at relatives who hinted at "the spectrum." Weren't we all somewhere on that spectrum? Dan wondered what would happen with his son post-divorce … if it came to that.

***

Dan entered the church through the main door and found the upstairs empty. He proceeded to the basement, one careful step at a time. At the bottom landing, Dan's heart quickened and he arrested his forward motion. A woman in jeans and a blue smock, no doubt the custodian, stood before him giving him the fisheye. Maybe it was Dan's attire—an old gray hoodie with the hood shrouding his face.

"What you looking for? The meeting?"

Dan segued into his cover story. "Well, yeah, but what I really need is a bathroom." Met by more fisheye. "It's urgent or I wouldn't—"

The woman motioned with her chin. "End of the hall, past the meeting room."

Ahead, the door to the meeting room stood ajar. Not a situation Dan wanted, but with the custodian at his back, he had no choice but to tighten his hood and step into no-man's-land. His passing peripheral revealed fifteen or twenty people sitting on chairs in a circle holding hands, heads bowed—nobody looking his way. In the men's room, Dan took a breath and used the toilet. He washed his hands, dallied a minute, then returned to the gauntlet, beginning to wish he hadn't started this venture.

The custodian was gone, enabling Dan to edge along the wall toward the meeting room door. Two attendees came into view—still holding hands with bowed heads. Further steps displayed the rest of the group, including Shannon. On her left, she clasped the hand of another woman, but her starboard partner was a guy with red hair. Gaining the far side of the meeting room, Dan bounded up the basement stairs and retreated from the church. So, yes, she was at a meeting. But who was that guy? Dan crossed Fifth Avenue and stood behind parked cars midway between two dim street-lights.

A half-hour later, the meeting participants dribbled down the stone steps of the church, Shannon alongside the red-headed guy. They turned north and walked up the block together, with Dan shadowing them from across the avenue. At the corner, they stopped, faced each other, and hugged. A brief hug, less than two seconds, but there it was. He heard Shannon say. "Night, Woody."

Woody. The man turned west, while Shannon continued north. Dan crossed Fifth, concocting strategy on the fly. Should he go after his wife? No, he'd see her later at the apartment, and manliness mandated accosting the interloper. As Dan followed the bobbing red coiffure, a distressing picture played upon his mind. He envisioned Woody's bare buttocks between his wife's—oh, wicked wench! Oh, let her rot and perish and be damned! And for this meddler, black vengeance calls!

On the far side of Sixth Avenue, Dan closed upon his antagonist, their footfalls in sync on the dark sidewalk. Cement stoops to the left, green bags of garbage on the street side. Nothing attended Dan's mind but outrage. No reason, no contemplation, no worry about jumping to a faulty conclusion; just rage. His hands rose (as of their own accord), elbows bent, palms out, located the red-haired man's scapulae, and pushed.

A second of impulse, with no plan and little forethought. Over in a second, but for the consequences. Woody stumbled, caught his balance, and turned sideways. Dan's momentum carried his upper chest into his adversary's biceps. He wrapped his arms around the larger (he now realized) man; the duet lurched and twirled along the edge of the sidewalk in an arrhythmic tango. Green plastic approached Dan's face as he and his opponent lost their vertical deportment. They bounced off a 20-gallon garbage bag and rolled into the street. Dan's glasses came askew, one temple in place behind his ear, the other unhinged. A metallic, salty tang breached his mouth. As he identified the taste as blood, a pink-nosed mammal of the order *Rodentia* sniffed its way toward his face. The skew of his glasses magnified the size of the beast and elicited a howl.

"Fucking rat!"

"Fucking rat yourself," Woody said, still tight in Dan's embrace.

Dan rolled from his side to his back, his opponent atop him, struggled back to his side, and flipped again to his back. Dan's outrage subsided, replaced by embarrassment at his situation and dread that he'd made a profound error in judgment; maybe several. Time receded. Seconds and minutes felt like hours. Grunts and groans, interspersed with expletives, Dan fearful of releasing his grip.

"Hey. Hey, knock it off."

The shouts came from above. Dan turned his head and through the misalignment of his glasses discerned two shiny black shoes and two blue pant legs. And behind the pant legs, the out-of-focus throbbing of blue lights over a white car. The legs flexed at the knees, and a uniformed cop lowered his lanky frame into a squat. He had soft brown skin, soft brown eyes, and a tranquil voice.

"What are you boys doing?"

Concurrent with the tall cop's query, a shorter cop, flashing in and out of the strobing blue of the patrol car, addressed his radio. "Yeah, you hoid me. Two middle-age white guys."

At the tall cop's urging, the combatants rose to their feet, Dan's glasses at a ten-degree angle. The cop directed Woody toward the patrol car to commune with his partner. Once they were alone, he said to Dan, "Now, what's this all about?"

Dan groped for words, uttering what stumbled into his head. "I just, well, I bumped into him by accident, totally by accident, and next thing we're on the ground. He just attacked me. Just like that."

"Wait here, please."

As the tall cop retired toward the patrol car, Galaxy Bells announced an incoming call. Dan fished his phone from his pocket—Shannon—and swiped.

"Look … I'm afraid something happened while I was out walking … no, no, just walking around, getting some exercise, ha ha, but I tripped over a curb … dumb … yeah, yeah, they should put in better lights … anyhow, I hurt my face … I'll call you back in a few minutes … that noise, yeah, some people stopped to help me."

Dan stashed his phone as the tall cop returned.

"So, sir. The other gentleman involved in this altercation has given me a story that diverges from yours in several particulars. In fact, he suggests you were the aggressor."

The cop scanned the street up and down. "It's unfortunate we don't have any cameras around here. So, without those forensics—"

On the sidewalk, a dog approached—a black lab, attached to a leash held by a retirement-age woman. "Is everything all right, officer?"

"Yes, ma'am, a minor affair."

"We don't usually get riffraff around here."

"Right, ma'am. Very minor. No danger to the public."

At the lab's insistence, the woman moved on.

"So, sir," the tall cop said. "Looking at your face, I'd say you're the more aggrieved party. Do you wish to file a complaint?"

"A complaint?"

"Right, a formal complaint. Names, addresses, go before the judge. Because if you do, we have to get going on the paperwork."

"That's a lot of complication."

"It is. And that's how the other party feels, but like I say, you're more aggrieved."

As Dan shook his head, the short cop yelled into his radio. "Looks like we're gonna toin them loose."

"Do you want an ambulance?" said the tall cop, peering at Dan's face. "An escort to emergency? Your call, but your face is a mess."

***

Dan sat at the kitchen table. Shannon stood over him and dabbed his face with a wad of gauze. Ryan sat across from his step-father, elbows on the table, chin on his folded hands.

"Hold still," Shannon said. She dabbed again. "You know, it's not that bad once you get the blood cleared away."

"My glasses are broken." Dan had a backup pair, but with an outdated prescription.

"They're just bent," Ryan said. "I can fix them."

Shannon stopped dabbing to examine her son. "Why are you wearing that towel like it's a cape?"

"I'm getting down with *Othello*." A green bath towel with vertical white stripes, secured at the neck with a black binder clip, size large, from Staples. Dan took notice, but was more concerned with his own situation than another ripple in Ryan's behavior. So what if he wanted to get down with *Othello*? What had he said about the glasses?

"Othello wore a cape?" Shannon said.

"Actually, I'm Iago. They all did back then."

Shannon shook her head and resumed swabbing Dan's face.

Dan said, "I'll have to bring them to Warby."

"There's one in Grand Central."

"Dad," Ryan said, "it's nothing to fix them." He snatched the plastic-framed glasses from the kitchen table and stood with a flourish of his towel-cape. Two strides carried him to the kitchen sink, where he immersed the bent temple under hot water.

"What are you doing?" Dan said.

"Making them pliable." Ryan turned off the water and grasped the glasses between thumbs and forefingers. A bend here, a twist there, and he handed them to his father. To Dan's amazement, the repaired glasses slid over his nose and ears like an optometrist had fitted them.

Ryan stared into Dan's face. "Looking good. So, Dad, do you mind a personal question?"

"How personal?"

"Are you smoking anything?"

"Ryan," Shannon said.

Dan put on his aggrieved voice. "Why would you say that?"

"It's kind of suspicious. You go out for a quote-unquote walk and come back after tripping over yourself."

"It's the city," Shannon said, "with their crappy street lights. We may even have a lawsuit."

"Anyways." Ryan pulled his towel-cape around his torso. "I have to swoop back to my studies."

"Swoop away," Shannon said, and turned to her husband's face. She abandoned the gauze in favor of a moist washcloth. A few seconds passed.

Dan said, "Do you guys do huggy stuff at your meetings?"

"Oh, tell me about it. Sometimes it's too much. Hold still. Some of them … they don't mean anything … they just overdo it. Wasn't Iago the villain?"

"Kind of. Some people think he was a stand-in for the dark side of human nature."

"Okay, professor. Here's another question. Should our son be running around with a towel flapping behind him? I mean, he's eighteen."

"He's a visionary, like Einstein. Visionaries are sometimes un-orthodox."

"Didn't Einstein marry his first cousin? Hold still. Not to be judgmental. Just saying."

***

A week later, Dan lay on the living room couch, his glasses off, a damp washcloth across his face, at the tail end of milking his injuries. Shannon sat alongside him.

She said, "These meetings mean a lot to me. I'll be back in two and a half hours."

"I know." Dan was past imagining the worst and still shaken by his close call with infamy. He wanted to consign to oblivion what had occurred, not to mention what could have occurred.

Shannon leaned over and puckered her lips. Dan reciprocated.

"Ryan is here if you need anything."

"I know."

He'd resolved to take a philosophical approach to Shannon's Wednesday night meetings; had decided they were what they appeared to be and were good for her. As Shannon closed the apartment door behind her, Dan sat up and reached across the coffee table for the latest *New Yorker*. He put on his glasses and flipped to the cartoon caption contest on the penultimate page. Two and a half hours passed. Dan had examined all the cartoons in the magazine, back to front, read the lead article under The Talk of the Town, and slogged through two feature articles. He was trying to take an interest in the fiction piece when the apartment door reopened. Shannon flung off her coat and scurried onto the couch next to Dan.

"You won't believe this. One of our guys, Woody. We call him that because of his red hair. Like Woody Woodpecker." She chuckled. "A joke."

Dan tossed aside the *New Yorker* and faced his wife's torrent of words.

"After the meeting last week, he got assaulted in the street. On the sidewalk, actually, but it went into the street. Assault and battery. Can you believe that? In the Village, between Sixth and Seventh."

"Wow."

"He beat the guy off. This guy was big, half a head taller, Woody said, but he beat him off. Although Fred—he's another regular—said the only thing Woody could beat off was his you-know-what."

Dan joined Shannon in a short laugh.

"Then the cops showed up. Good thing for the other guy, said Woody, or he would have done some real damage." Shannon gave Dan's chest a quick slap. "Hey, that was the same night you fell down. I wonder what's happening next."

"Next?"

"Yeah. Everything happens in threes, and it's Wednesday night again. Oh, look."

Along with Shannon, Dan looked down.

"I didn't even take off my shoes."

Shannon walked back to the front door and kicked off her shoes. On the return trip, she jumped to a sudden bang. Dan stiffened before realizing the noise was Ryan's door being flung open and striking the wall. Ryan stepped from the hallway and advanced. He wore his green towel-cape with white stripes, secured at the neck by the black, size large, binder clip from Staples. His chest was bare. On his lower torso—

"Are those my panties?" Shannon said. They were. Her red Chantelle Soft Stretch, now sporting a ballet bulge at the groin.

Ryan leveled his right arm at his father, forefinger extended. His lips formed an orb like the top of a volcano. "O beware, my lord, of jealousy." His finger and eyes turned skyward. "It is the green-eyed monster which doth mock the meat it feeds on."

"Ryan, take off my panties. No, not here."

"Gee, Mom, make up your mind. What do you think, Dad?"

Dan wet his lips with his tongue. "You might be overacting."

Ryan looked at his mother.

"Definitely overacting," she said.

"Hmm." With a swish of his towel-cape, Ryan turned on his right heel.

"My God," Shannon said, following her son's egress.

"Did they catch the guy, or anything?" Dan said.

"What guy?"

"The one who attacked what's-his-name."

"Oh, Woody, yeah. Like I said, the cops came. Can you believe that? In New York City, a cop shows up when you need one."

Dan shook his head.

"But Woody didn't press charges. Too much trouble. He should have, though."

"Why's that?"

"Why? You never know about those guys. Next thing, he's pushing people in front of a train."

"Good point."

"You know, you should come with me some Wednesday night. Meet the gang." Shannon fell back on the couch, laughing. "You should see your face."

"It's just that—"

"I know, no touchy-feely for you." Shannon laughed again.

She stared into her husband's countenance. "Almost like new."

Samuel
Hoffmann

Waiting to Story,

My book slept on the floor today

Propped like a tent, pages folded over,
the spine slowly cracking open
A casualty of an unlucky flip off the bed
and the uncontrollable force of gravity

Misplaced, compared to pristine bookshelves
free housing too full,
empty apartments questioning cost
this story has no home, no shelf

Outcast by a society too busy
untaxed donations replace attention
as free bookmark charities hide
streets of Homelessness

Nameless, this cardboard covered book
begs its now ordinary cry for love
and for a shelf with companions to lean on

Kris Kaila

Night Stroll

I see them through the window his mouth
    open
        words devouring
he sucking out her spirit
as she shrinks
    and bends.
his spit
    like darts
going
    all
        around
    the
target.

the tightness in his jaw
eyes squeezed tight
and I know
she is counting

in
her
head
trying to
      deflect
         the
            blows.
if they miss their target
     game over

his hands once clenched at his sides thrust out
     around her.

     she flinches
even when she can't see them he's
     pacing as
she sways
slowly backs up to the wall
staring at one another
chests heaving
mouths open

between my thumb and forefinger I pinch his head
wishing I could pop his overripe reddened face
and peel her like a sticker
off the wall

Guorong Zhu

Chicago Marathon: Run for Those Who Can't

The real purpose of running isn't to win a race. It's to test the limits of the human heart.

  —Bill Bowerman, track & field coach and co-founder of Nike

At precisely 5:00 a.m., three alarms went off in a Chicago hotel room. The two iPhones sang in contrasting tunes—one soothing "Silk," the other jarring "Radar"—while an insistent buzz emanated from the hotel nightstand's alarm clock. The darkness shattered into a million irregular pieces.

Before I could snooze my phone, Chuan flicked on the overhead light. She released a deep sigh and lamented, "I couldn't fall back to sleep after waking up at 1:00 a.m."

"How do you feel now?" I inquired as a muted voice flashed through my mind, pondering how the lack of sleep would affect her. We had aimed for the perfect 8-hour pre-race sleep—lights off at 8:30, conk out at 9:00, wake up refreshed at 5:00—a plan it seemed only one of us managed to execute appropriately.

"Min-Min updated us on WeChat at 1:00 a.m." Chuan deflected my question. "Her flight was delayed."

Min-Min was going to share the hotel bed with me last night. At the 2022 Mount Washington Road Race, she shared a hotel room with me and got to appreciate my trademark talent: sleeping. I had built a reputation for sleeping like a log—no midnight awakenings, no snoring, and no tossing and turning. Once I drifted into slumber, I practically ceased to exist, making me the ideal roommate for runners.

Months before the application window for a non-guaranteed entry into the 2023 Bank of America Chicago Marathon opened, Chuan secured a strategically located hotel room. When the notification arrived on December 8, 2022, Min-Min and I were unexpectedly selected. We implored Chuan to share her room, closest to both the start and finish lines, as "bedmates."

My bedmate Min-Min and I took the same flight to Chicago Midway Airport. We landed yesterday and immediately headed to a carb-loading lunch organized by BEN, a running group of Chinese Americans in the Greater Boston Area. Having arrived earlier, Chuan had already picked up her bib from the expo. All three of us, members of BEN, ran together weekly along the Charles River or Minuteman Bike Path. This was the first Chicago Marathon for all of us.

The BEN lunch took place at MingHin Cuisine in Chicago Chinatown on the first floor, while a group of Beijing University Alumni runners were also carb-loading upstairs. As an alumna and invited to both gatherings, I ran back and forth between floors to participate in group pictures for both events and did not get to eat much.

Min-Min did not eat at all. Sitting at the BEN table, she clutched her phone to her ear, jotting notes on a napkin, eyebrows furrowed, and forehead creased.

"The scallion pancake is still warm," I offered, pushing the plate towards Min-Min when she finally hung up.

She didn't glance at the food but met my eyes. "My dad had a stroke." Tears welled up. "I need to go back to Boston now."

Her delayed flight landed in Boston at 1:00 a.m. on Sunday, October 8, the day of the Chicago Marathon, the race we had been training for since July.

Waking up on race day without Min-Min in bed, I exclaimed, "Bathroom first," reciting from the day's timetable, now that Min-Min had left, leaving Chuan and me to follow.

"I already went," Chuan admitted sheepishly, evidently feeling guilty for deviating from the plan.

"We can't eat the bagels yet!" I shouted while sitting on the toilet, trying to feel any signs of bowel movement.

Yesterday, Min-Min carried a bag of Costco bagels from Boston, following advice from the so-called "runner's bible" *Advanced Marathoning*: "Avoid consuming foods that are known to cause digestive discomfort." Costco bagels from Boston were our safest carb-loading choice. There were six in the bag, and we were each going to eat two at 6:00 a.m.

Even before consuming any food, my digestive system was already stressed out, now that I commanded it to empty all waste on Chicago time. Still, there are no signs of a bowel movement. Concentrate. Meditate. Remember, everything is psychological. You must have faith: see it, believe it, and make it happen! I delivered a motivational speech to myself while seated on the toilet.

Coming out of the bathroom with the first success checked off, I noticed that Chuan had already donned her running outfit, nearly identical to what I had laid out on the sofa the night before: a high-impact bra for running, a tech tee, shorts with phone pockets stuffed with energy gels, compression long socks, race shoes, and, most importantly, the Garmin watch. Nothing more, not even underwear. A Chinese proverb says that carrying a feather could wear you down during a long-distance run.

A chill ran down my spine when I left the hotel at 7:00 a.m. The temperature was 43 degrees, "feels like 41," according to my Garmin watch. The plastic trash bag on top of my ex-husband's sweater did not block out the cold air as expected. Michigan Avenue was flooded with people walking speedily in the same direction. Chuan and I joined the current toward the start line.

Grant Park unfurled like a picnic blanket between Chicago skyscrapers and Lake Michigan. Waves and corrals of runners formed its plaid print. Thousands of runners were chatting, fidgeting, drinking water, and eating energy gels. I did not hear any announcement or the firing of the race start gun. When suddenly the crowd started to move, I shed the trash bag and my ex-husband's sweater, threw them away, and joined the flowing current, shoulder to shoulder with Chuan.

The race thus began, not as ceremonial as I had envisioned. Run. One foot in front of another. I could sense the soles of my shoes contacting the paved road, my heart synchronizing with the rhythmic beats. *I am running the Chicago Marathon!*

Seven lanes merged into a tunnel, demanding an adjustment from my eyes. A curious sight awaited on either side of the road: a fence of buttocks displaying a spectrum of hues from white and yellow to brown and black. My instinct to reach for my phone to capture the moment was thwarted by the realization that I had chosen not to bring my phone to the race to avoid extra weight.

"I want to pee too." Chuan suddenly declared beside me.

"No," I countered. "You don't need to pee." We had used the portable toilet minutes ago. "You may think you need to pee, but you don't."

Emerging from the tunnel, the echoes dissipated beside my ears. Now, the predominant sound was the symphony of footsteps, resembling the thunderous gallop of thousands of horses. The rhythm became disordered when approaching hydration stations.

Everything is psychological. The ultimate test of endurance is how long you can hold your bladder—a measure of discipline and health, both physical and mental. Concentrate! Put one foot in front of the other.

I told Chuan that I did 10 years of executive assessment at a headhunter company, administering batteries of tests on high-flying and even higher-flying executives for C-suite jobs. These job candidates were tested for every capability: intellectual, physical, social, and emotional. I thought we had exhausted all conceivable tests, mainly to make sure our recommendations would be legally defendable in court, even though all measures ultimately could boil down to one: the duration a person could hold their bladder.

Chuan and I maintained bladder control at each hydration station. One to two miles apart, volunteers were handing out small cups of Gatorade or water along both sides of the course. We didn't skip a single station. Our registration fee covered the cost, an amount that could have easily procured us 10 tons of water.

Suddenly, a runner on my right raised both arms, signaling fervently. Turning, I spotted a camera lens the size of a side-dish plate nestled between her arms. Photo op! A nearby sign humorously reminded me: "Smile! You paid for this." I stuck out my tongue, attempting the biggest BEN signature smile, only to have it obscured by the man in front of me who leaned back to insert his head into the camera. I couldn't help but wonder if he was one of the infamous "6.2 Most Annoying People You'll Encounter While

Running a Race" (https://www.levelman.com/annoying-people-running-marathon).

The course twisted and turned. Just 4 miles in, I had lost count of the lefts and rights. I endeavored to pass on the left, seemingly the rightful path. "Follow the blue line," I recalled reading about the Chicago Marathon. "It is the most direct, fastest way to the finish line." Yet passing on left turns felt akin to cutting the corner.

"Time to eat one energy gel," Chuan announced.

"How many energy gels will we need in total?" I reached into the pockets on both sides of my shorts to recount the number of gels stashed there.

"It depends on how fast you run. Take one every 40 minutes."

"How fast should I run?" We did not get to discuss this before the race.

"What is your goal?" She looked at me, puzzled.

"A PR?" I was tentative.

Chuan finished her first marathon last fall in 4:34. earlier this spring, my inaugural marathon, aptly named the Cheap Marathon —with a $26.20 entry fee, no water station, no medal, only a really cheap finisher ribbon—was completed in 4:26.

"Given how slow we were, a PR is not a challenging goal," Chuan said. "Even if we finish the Chicago Marathon one second faster, it'll be our PR."

"So, my goal is to finish in 4 hours and 25 minutes," I declared, "A PR by a whole minute!"

"If we can finish in under 4:20, we will qualify for next year's Chicago marathon, and then we can accompany Min-Min for her deferred race." Remarkably, Chuan spoke this lengthy sentence without slowing down her pace, and I could feel her words sinking in one syllable at a time without missing a beat.

Suddenly, I had a goal—a clear, bold number: 4 hours and 20 minutes, which would qualify me to accompany Min-Min for the Chicago Marathon 2024.

"Let's go for it!" I exclaimed, my voice rising with enthusiasm.

"Would you two stop talking?!" A sharp voice, punctuated by the woman's heavy breathing, sliced through the air from behind us. I turned around to find a lady about my age glaring at us with a puffed face. I wondered how long she had been trailing us, not fast enough to pass us yet unwilling to slow down. Our banter must have cut through her like a knife, exacerbating the agony settling in from every muscle, joint, tendon, and brain cell five miles into the race.

Chuan and I shut up.

Running our first official marathon, we felt like two country girls at the Met Gala: unsure of the theme, uncertain of our fashion sense, hesitant with our manners, and afraid to offend. I especially did not want others to form a bad impression of Chinese runners even though we were not the only "yellow faces," and we did not have representation obligations besides the bright red shirts we were wearing, sponsored by a Chinese sportswear company.

We ran in silence and dared not to turn our heads, unsure if the lady demanding our silence still trailed us, even during pit stops at hydration stations for water or Gatorade. The "8 miles" sign passed in silence without a word exchanged between Chuan and me.

Suddenly, a phone rang, and the woman ahead of us abruptly halted to answer, shattering the monotony of footsteps and our silence. A multitude of thoughts raced through my mind. "Who the hell is calling?" I mused. "It's probably not a call from hell because hell is right here, in the middle of running a marathon. It better be God. But I wouldn't pick up, even if God is calling."

As a courtesy, Chuan and I halted, too.

Before I could catch my breath, the woman exclaimed, "A new world record is set!" What? Did someone finish the race while I still have 17 miles to go?

As the thought dashed through my mind, I spotted a spectator's sign proclaiming, "The Kenyans are already done."

"What's the new world record?" I asked Chuan, not expecting her to have the answer. The sheer wonder of the possibility spurred us onward: "Could it possibly be under 2 hours?"

No matter what, it felt as though the divine forces of the marathon gods were at play. Chuan and I paid our respects by consuming another energy gel while waiting for the news-reporting runner to stow her phone. We resumed our pace.

A pacer breezed by, brandishing a 4:20 sign.

Should I follow him? What's his pace? Let me do the math. To finish in 4:20, the pace must be 9:55 minutes per mile or 6:10 minutes per kilometer. No, I can't do that. My last long run with Min-Min was at 10:23 minutes per mile. 9:55 would be way too much of a leap for me.

"What is the qualification time for the Chicago Marathon?" I asked Chuan again.

"4:20."

But to accompany Min-Min for 2024, we needed to finish in under 4 hours and 20 minutes.

Wait, how did the 4:20 pacer overtake me? Am I already lagging as I started before him? Does that mean even if I follow his pace from now on, there is no guarantee I will finish the race in under 4:20...

Too many thoughts were bumping into each other in my mind, like all the runners I bumped into, slowing down again to grab a cup of water on the side. Meanwhile, the 4:20 pacer surged down the course on the blue line without stopping for water.

Runners streamed past me on both sides. "Go, hotdog!" Some spectators cheered from their front porch as a man in a costume zoomed by on my left. How can he run so swiftly in that gigantic balloon? I wondered, acknowledging that my chances of finishing under 4:20 were slipping away with every passing moment.

A church bell rang, piercing through my thoughts. *Is it 9 o'clock or 10? Are we at mile 11, 12, or 13? Regardless, I must be traversing the Old Town of Chicago.*

"Don't rush." Chuan patted my swinging arm. "We need to reserve energy for the second half."

"Negative split?" I recalled hearing the phrase somewhere. Experienced marathon runners finish the second half faster than the first.

"Yes." Chuan nodded. "Looks like you are in great condition to do so."

Along the street, restaurants and cafes bordered commercial and residential buildings, red brick blending with grey cement and glass set in wooden and metal frames. Diners filled outdoor tables adorned with checkered tablecloths. Some relished morning coffee and pastries, while others enjoyed hot lunches.

"Go, runners!" The clinking of glasses resonated with cheers, and their drinks sparkled like liquid sunshine.

The scents of freshly brewed coffee mixed with the unmistakable sizzle of grilled meats made me hungry. I reached into my pocket for a caffeinated gel.

Chuan pulled out her gel, about to tear it open, but stopped mid-air and said, "Feel free to follow her if you want to."

She pointed to a pacer passing us from behind, holding a 4:10 sign. *Is she the 4:10 pacer for our corral or for later ones?* My brain cells refused to connect.

"Shi Jie (school sister)!" I cried out in Chinese, recognizing the pacer from yesterday's Beijing University alumni lunch, though her name escaped me. She had graduated five years earlier than me.

She was running in a bright red T-shirt with Beijing University on the back.

She turned around without slowing, flashed a big smile, and said "Follow me" in Chinese.

Should I?

Chuan nodded. "Go ahead." Her eyes sparkled. "You are faster than me."

I gave Chuan's hand a squeeze, felt the warmth of her skin, pumped my arms harder, and dashed to the side of Shi Jie.

The next miles went by as if I had turned on a mechanical mode. All I did was stay behind Shi Jie and follow the rhythm of her movement. "Clap, clap, clap…" Her feet beat the ground like a Chinese zither, and the pluck of each step became my rhythmic heartbeat. The tempo was not hasty but steady, akin to the measured tick of a metronome, *Metronomic cadence, a marathoner's dance.* I suddenly felt a poetic rush.

A handful of people followed Shi Jie, running toward the same goal held in her hand: 4:10. Even though no one spoke, I felt synchronized with the group in our breathing. The same air flowed in and out of our lungs, circulating in an invisible bubble.

"Pick up your feet!" Shi Jie shouted, taking a right turn onto a bridge. What is this? I jumped more at the sight of red carpets covering the grates on the bridge than at the change of texture on the surface. An experienced pacer, Shi Jie didn't seem to change her pace at all.

I tried to keep up, especially after I stopped for water. *I know it's psychological, but I must stop for water!* Shi Jie never stopped at the hydration stations; she carried her own water. I asked why. She said as a pacer, she had to maintain a very consistent pace. Given the number of runners following her, not everyone was stopping at the same hydration station, so she had to skip them all. "But I will stop at the Chinatown hydration station," she said. She added that over 200 Chinese volunteers would be there, serving water and Gatorade, providing medical aid, and taking pictures. There would be a bright red Beijing University flag for the proud alumni runners.

I heard the banging gongs and drums first; then came the bright red flags hoisting giant golden characters streaking through the air. Finally came the dancing lions, winking at me as they sneaked across the cheering crowds of yellow faces. *Chinatown!*

The Chinatown hydration station was a seemingly endless sea of waving hands and enthusiastic smiles. Dotted among the crowds, grey-uniformed Asian volunteers lined both sides of the street, handing out Gatorade and water. Bursting through the cacophonous cheers, a sudden eruption of voices called out towards me, "Jin, Jin! Look here, Jin!" Bewildered, I turned around, pointing at myself and thinking, "Me? I am not Jin!?"

Then, my previously constant companion Shi Jie left my side and darted towards the crowd, embracing them over the hydration table. The warm welcome was not for me. It was for my pacer, Jin, whom I had been calling Shi Jie (school sister) for miles.

Jin resumed her pace after hugging the group, which, I later learned, were members of Chi, the Chinese running club of Chicago. She posed for pictures several times with different flags, all striking red, without missing a beat through Chinatown.

I struggled to keep up.

My big toe started to throb. It was a problem that could run in my family. For three decades, my grandma endured the grotesque ancient practice of foot-binding, leaving her big toe bent upwards, the other four tucked beneath, forming the infamous "three-inch golden lotus." Grandma's 94-year-long life, despite being filled with numerous joys, saw no running, a freedom she lost at the early age of 4. My mom freed her feet soon after the establishment of the People's Republic of China in 1949, but bunions had already developed outside of her big toes, and her feet were too deformed to walk long distances.

I, on the other hand, was fortunate enough to escape foot-binding. I wore standard-sized shoes, could crisscross shopping malls for hours, and got to jog alongside my children as I taught them how to bike. Yet by the third hour of the Chicago Marathon, the bony bump outside my big toe, where the foot-binding practices would have targeted, began to flare up.

Each lift-off and landing of my foot sent a sharp radiating sting up from the bony bump. The pain journeyed through my calf, thigh, pelvis, and trunk, resonating up to my scalp, akin to an electric wave coursing through my entire being. Biting down, I knew I couldn't stop running. This race was bigger than me. I was also running for my mom and my grandma, who were deprived of their chance to run.

Why am I subjecting myself to this? What purpose does it serve? I recalled the initial conversation with my mom about participating in the Chicago Marathon. Her inquiry was straightforward, "How much are you getting paid for running the race?" *The truth is no one compensated me for enduring this hardship. I paid for the pain and exhaustion.*

Sweat oozed from my forehead, merged into big drops, rolled over my eyebrows, and blurred my vision. I wiped my eyes with the back of my hand. Amidst the exertion, a sign caught my attention, its bold words urging, "Don't Run," followed by the punch line, "for yourself. Run for someone who can't."

Who can't? The words immediately directed my thoughts to Min-Min, currently tending to her father in a hospital bed. My thoughts extended to my late father, who departed years ago, and my grandmother, whose ability to run was stripped away at the tender age of 4. In that moment, the realization struck me: I ran for them, for those who couldn't experience the freedom of running.

Beyond Chinatown, the crowd dispersed, and the road widened before me. Peering ahead, a lengthy straight road unfolded, populated by runners nearing mile marker 24 on the opposite side. This stretch marked one of those sections where the course looped back upon itself, yet I couldn't spot Jin and her 4:10 sign on either side of the course.

A surreal sensation enveloped me as if time had decelerated, and the surroundings melded into a haze. My senses were reduced to the cadence of my breathing, short and labored. To regain composure, I attempted the odd-numbered breathing technique, inhaling on counts of 1-2-3-4 and exhaling on 5-6-7.

Hydration stations appeared at regular intervals, offering not only Gatorade and water but also sliced bananas, each segment with its peel on. Yellow banana skins littered the pavement, transitioning from bright to black, creating a treacherous, sticky terrain underfoot.

I recalled Peter Sagal's *The Incomplete Book of Running*, penned by the host of my favorite NPR program, "Wait, Wait, Don't Tell Me." The Studebaker Theater in the Fine Arts Building, close to the Chicago Marathon's starting line, hosted live tapings of Sagal's show.

Sagal was twice a Boston Marathon finisher as a guide for blind runners. This prompted me to ponder the challenges visually impaired runners might face with the littered banana peels of the Chicago Marathon.

Struggling amidst slippery banana peels and contemplative musings, I turned onto the return leg, now on the side where I had previously seen the 24-mile sign. Exhaustion set in, draining me of the energy to grasp for another energy gel. Thirst persisted, yet I hesitated to pause for water. The only directive echoing in my mind: keep running, one foot in front of the other.

The throng of spectators swelled. As the finish line loomed into view, a cascade of emotions crashed through me: relief, then a surge of profound emotion, followed by another wave of relief. Arms raised high, I sprinted over the electric band.

I ran into Jin's open arms. She was waiting for me at the finish line, still holding the 4:10 sign. "You made it!" she screamed.

Gasping for air, I squeaked out: "Was… I… under 4:20?"

Before she could answer, a man ran over to Jin and, with one arm wrapped around her and the other holding a 3:20 sign, beamed, "Hey, I'm Jin's husband. What does your Garmin say?" What a power couple, both pacing the same race!

We looked together—my Garmin stopped at 4:17:53. I qualified!

Then, I caught sight of Chuan as she passed through. "Am I the one-millionth runner?" she asked in good spirits.

Confused, I queried, "What one-millionth runner?"

Unbeknownst to me, the Chicago Marathon 2023 had planned to celebrate its 45-year history with a celebratory recognition of the symbolic one-millionth finisher. "If I can't be first, I might as well be the millionth," Chuan exclaimed, chuckling at her finish time of 4:19:48.

"No. You were too fast," Jin quipped back playfully.

Min-Min, best of luck to your father.

Chuan and I burst out in unison. "Let's run the 2024 Chicago Marathon together!"

Mary D.
Chaffee

Honey in My Mouth

The whole family lives in a little blue house
With no straight lines

On a rag rug in front of the hearth
An old dog smiles in her sleep
White polka-dot curtains divide the round window – just one!

He sits in an overstuffed armchair, pea green
The one with the ragged places carefully darned
In yellow cotton thread (it was all they had)
Sitting back, he sips a cup of
Chamomile tea and sighs a little

In bear country
It is always fall
The colored leaves drop gently, maple and poplar
Dogwood and birch

A red brick path winds away to
Woodcut hills

Will I ever again come down that old familiar way
The scent of September fields like
Honey in my mouth?

Jim Wyman

Nearly Forever

Every summer
Her expansive leaf-filled limbs
Would shade us
Like the inviting arms
Of a doting aunt without children of her own.

There
At the river's bend
We would swing from her corded rope
Practice holding on
Then
Letting go
And
With the wild abandonment of youth
Fling ourselves
Farther and farther
Into deeper and deeper water.

Nearly one lifetime later
I returned
Walked with familiar footing
Passed remembered trees
With carved hearts and initials
Only to find her gone.

Washed away
By a winding river
Searching for the sea.

Jim Wyman

An Alluvial View

Looking back
at the narrow canyon
of my youth
I have found all those sharp edges of body and mind
softly rounded
by the quickened pace of time.
Now
a gentle rhythm
has been found
on this leveled plain
of dreams fulfilled
I meander on.

Contributors

Sally Ballin wrote her first short story in second grade. It was a graphic novel about an Easter chicken from the chicken's point of view. From then on she was addicted to the short story form, but stopped illustrating them within a few years of the chicken story launch. Since then, she has written numerous short stories, a play, and a novel in and around raising a family, earning a living, doing volunteer work, folding laundry, and so forth. Now she is working on the story of her family for her grandchildren, of which her *Cold Lake Anthology* selection is one piece.

Edward Baran writes out of Somers, New York. A retired actor with degrees in religion, he now writes of things he has learned and things he has been given.

Charles Belson (cover art) is an American architect, artist, author, and photographer. His watercolor for the cover of *Cold Lake Anthology 2024* explores the theme of reflections, as does his 2023 book *Reflections: An Architect's Memoir*. Belson's work also has appeared in *Connecticut Literary Anthology, Period Homes Magazine, Hamilton Magazine,* and *The New York Times*. A graduate of Yale and Harvard, he lives in Connecticut. belsondesign.com/firm/publicationsvideos.html

A lifelong New Englander, **Jeff Bernstein** watches the seasons turn from a hillside in central Vermont. He would like to have been, like Thoreau, "an inspector of snow-storms and rain-storms… [a] surveyor, if not of highways, then of forest paths and all across-lot routes." His new collection, *The Ancient Ways*, will be published in 2024 by Aldrich Press. He was runner-up in the 2023 Concrete Wolf Louis Poetry Book Award. Other poems have recently appeared or will appear shortly in, among other publications, *Abandoned Mine*, *The MacGuffin*, *Portrait of New England*, *Sleet*, and *Trestle Ties*.

Anne Bower teaches tai chi, gardens, enjoys community volunteering, and keeps writing. Publications include three chapbooks: *Poems for Tai Chi Players* (Kattywompus Press), *The Space Between Us* (Finishing Line Press), and *Getting It Down on Paper* (co-author Pamela Ahlen; Orchard Street Press). Poems have appeared in *Likely Red, Naugatuck River Review, ArtAscent, Evening Street Review, Raven's Perch, Gemini, The Literary Nest, Plainsong*, and other journals and anthologies. Earlier in life, Anne taught American literature and composition at The Ohio State University-Marion and published in the field of food and culture.

Ana Burtnett feels whole when she is in the natural world, becoming aware of all her senses, emotions, and liminal places. Her poems remind the reader of a long-forgotten sensation, or an undisturbed memory, in order to uncover our more tender selves. Ana participates in the Burlington Writers Workshop's Poetry Feedback workshop, as well as the River Arts Poetry Clinic in Morrisville, Vermont. She has attended workshops hosted by Baron Wormser and Richard Blanco. Ana lives in beautiful Worcester, Vermont, where the natural world is just a footstep away. On Ana's nightstand currently: Jane Kenyon, Leo Dangle, Tony Hoagland, Billy Collins, Alison Prine, and Chard DeNiord.

Michelle Cacho-Negrete is a retired social worker who lives in Portland, Maine, but makes frequent visits to Burlington, Vermont. She has roughly 140 publications, four of which are among the most notable essays of the year and five of which are in anthologies. She is the author of *Stealing: Life in America.* She has won the Hope Award, was runner-up for the Brooklyn Literary Award, twice won Best of The Net, volunteers to help immigrant students with conversational English, and helped establish a speaking group to discuss women's history and rights for school groups.

Mary D. Chaffee doesn't really consider herself a poet, but sometimes one pops out without warning and is captured on whatever scrap of paper is handy, turning up much later in a pile and, occasionally, a publication. Devoted to writing horror fiction with a slice of wry, she coexists uneasily in Burlington, Vermont, with her partner and a clever, neurotic rescue pup called Peanut.

Ann Fisher lives in the foothills of Vermont's Green Mountains, though she is not the first, nor the last, to call that land home. She is the fiction co-editor for Mud Season Review. Ann's poetry and prose have appeared in *Zig Zag Lit Mag, About Place Journal, The South Shore Review, Plainsong,* and *MacQueen's Quinterly,* among others. Her work includes two nominations for the Pushcart Prize. www.annfishervt.com

Dennis Gray is a semi-retired videographer/photographer from Cincinnati, Ohio. He has previously published two books of poetry, *An Apology to a Fish* in 1979, and *Backroad Ramblings, Wayfarers' Verse* with Amy Hadley in 2022, which is a collection of photos and the poems they inspired. He is currently publishing a third book of poems entitled *Traps and Trappings of Love, Life and Left-handedness.*

Before he became a teacher at the age of 36, **David A. Hinkhouse** built new homes in and around Kansas City, Kansas. Building houses prepared him for teaching in many ways. He graduated from Kansas University with a degree in social studies education and received his MLA degree from Baker University. He ended up teaching high school and college English, along with taking on the myriad of other responsibilities that accompany those efforts. He has studied poetry with Leslie Ullman as his worthy and astute mentor. He has had a few poems published; in retirement, he pursues the craft of poetry as therapy and revelation.

Wendy Hoffman has published four memoirs: *The Enslaved Queen, White Witch in a Black Robe, A Brain of My Own,* and *After Amnesia. The Enslaved Queen* has been translated and published in Germany. Her book of poetry, *Forceps,* was published along with a book of essays, *From the Trenches,* written with Dr. Alison Miller. Her second poetry book, *Belonging,* published by Kelsay Books, has just been nominated for the Eric Hoffer Book Award. She does consultations for therapists working in the field of dissociative disorders.

Samuel Hoffmann grew up in New Jersey and graduated from Stony Brook University (New York). After college, he moved to Burlington, Vermont, where he works as a software developer and can be found biking, hiking, and snowboarding.

Whit Humphreys came to Vermont about 35 years ago after completing the Boston Museum School Program, with a focus on sculpture. His early days in Vermont were spent involved in The Carving Studio and quarries surrounding West Rutland. What attracted him to Vermont was the marble, the mountains, and a unique place to make art. He now lives in Benson, restoring old barns and beating back the burdock. He began writing poetry in 2021.

Kris Kaila is a Punjabi Canadian poet, writer, book reviewer, and blogger. She enjoys dabbling in visual art and cross-stitching/embroidery while drinking copious amounts of coffee or tea from her ever-growing mug collection. Her poetry has been published with Maza Arts Collective and in various anthologies and publications. Kris is a member of the League of Canadian Poets and the Federation of British Columbia Writers, and a Pushcart Prize nominee for 2023. On rainy days in beautiful Vancouver, British Columbia, if not writing Kris is usually volunteering for a writing organization, reading, or watching true crime documentaries. @krisesque_life (Instagram)

Tricia Knoll celebrates the publication of two poetry collections in 2024. *Wild Apples* highlights downsizing, moving 3,003 miles to Vermont, isolating during the pandemic, discovering Vermont, and welcoming two grandsons. *The Unknown Daughter* chapbook features poems by 27 different voices who react to the Tomb of the Unknown Daughter. The voices include the Daughter's mother, father, and brothers, neighbors, an Uber driver, the Watchwomen who protect the site, and more. Knoll is a contributing editor to the online journal *Verse Virtual.* Her work appears widely in journals and anthologies. triciaknoll.com

Sharon Lopez Mooney (1942-2024) was a retired Interfaith End of Life Chaplain who lived in Mexico and part-time in Northern California. Mooney received a California Arts Council Grant for rural poetry and co-published a local anthology. She's been a *Best of the Net* nominee and given *Editor's Choice* and *Elite Writer Status* honors. Her poetry collection *Cantata for a Desert Poet* was released January 2024 by Arteildoia Press. Mooney's poems, published nationally and internationally, appear in such publications as *New Verse News, Umbrella Factory, Visible Magazine, Muddy River Review, Revue {R}évolution, Avalon Literary, Ginosko, California Quarterly, Galway Review, Existere,* and *Adelaide International.* Her poems are indexed at sharonlopezmooney.com.

Bill Pendergraft founded Environmental Media in 1988, a company that writes, produces, and distributes media to support environmental education. He lives in Peacham, Vermont.

Robert Perron is the author of *The Blue House Raid,* a historical novel set in Korea. His short stories have appeared in various literary journals, such as *The Manchester Review, The Bombay Review,* and *Lowestoft Chronicle.* His past life includes high tech and military service. Visit his website at robertperron.com.

Kimberley Reynolds lives in Vermont's Mad River Valley, where she raised a family and continues her daily work of writing, editing, and management. She earned her MFA in Creative Writing from Emerson College and has a handful of personal essays published in various magazines. She attributes her close ties with her children and strong relationship with her husband for sustaining her writing and creative endeavors.

Robert Rosen has spent the better part of his life as a technologist and applied mathematician with a front-row seat to the technological revolutions of our time and the resulting social convulsions. He's written for the local newspaper in Vermont's Mad River Valley and has had a half-dozen stories published in speculative fiction magazines and music literary journals. He is currently working on his first novel, a story of our times set 2,500 years ago.

Born in Boston, **Lorraine Ryan** moved to Vermont, where she worked as a travel agent and real estate agent and owned a B&B with her husband and daughter. She was a program developer for University of Vermont Continuing Education and a freelance writer, and worked for Disney World in entertainment. When she and her husband bought a converted Greyhound bus, their lives expanded beyond the borders of New England and intersected with other travelers and residents. But writing was always the dream that flowed throughout her life. Besides hosting a Burlington Writers Workshop creative writing workshop, Lorraine is currently working on a children's book.

John Sanborn lives and works in Rutland, Vermont. He is a life-long Vermonter, is married to his college sweetheart, and brought up three daughters in Rutland. He has had many careers and enjoys the memories that underscore his poems.

Mary Schanuel has been a writer since she could hold a pencil and has published her work in newspapers, magazines, and journals since she was 18. Her fiction, poetry, and nonfiction works have appeared in the *New York Times, Los Angeles Daily News, Working Mother Magazine, Organic Gardening, Cold Lake Anthology, The Heartbeat, Feral: A Journal of Poetry and Art,*

FictionWeek Literary Review, *LifeSherpa*, St. Louis Public Radio, and others. She has written two novels, and her poetry and prose were featured in an anthology of Missouri writers called *In the Moment - Writing from a Spacious Mind.*

Cynthia Shepard grew up in northern Vermont. A country girl with an old creative soul, her interests are wide-ranging, with writing, scrapbooking, and knitting at the tip of the iceberg. Family traditions, a love of nature, and storytelling are the main themes that run through her art. She and her husband of 33 years have raised five children in the Lake Champlain Islands and have nine grandchildren so far. A natural multitasker, Cynthia finds her best ideas come to her amidst everyday activities.

Audrey Stibbe is new to writing and likes to write short stories that end with a twist. Poetry is her nemesis, but occasionally something clicks and her pen writes something weird and quirky. She lives on one of the Southern Gulf Islands off the coast of beautiful British Columbia, Canada, with her husband and 8-year-old rescue cat Priya. Her poem in *Cold Lake Anthology 2024* is her first publication and she is quite tickled. She would like to thank the Burlington Writers Workshop for its support and encouragement.

Candelin Wahl is a Vermont poet and songwriter. She has learned that a creative life requires saying YES to engagement with the wider world. Accepting social invites, exploring nature, cradling babies, taking road trips, making music with others—all sources of heart-opening inspiration. To read her published works, please visit candelinwahl.com.

Roger Watters started writing shortly after returning from Vietnam. He has written six books of poetry and a book of short stories. People, nature, and life experiences have kept the pen returning to the paper. His latest book of poetry is titled *Simple Thoughts*.

Julia Whinston is a bookseller and writer based in Winooski, Vermont. She has a degree in philosophy from the University of Maine and will soon be pursuing her masters at King's College London.

Jim Wyman is the last full-time resident on a one-lane, dirt, dead-end road at the tip of a long peninsula in the middle of a very large lake in northern Vermont. His poetry has been published in *Maya's Review: The Closed Eye Open*, *Ink In Thirds*, *Poem City*, and *Pegasus*, and has been displayed on the Poetry Path in Burlington, Vermont. He is the author of *Picture Perfect Poems* (Lulu.com/shop). Jim teaches at the Community College of Vermont.

Guorong Zhu is a management scholar and consultant whose academic journey took her from Beijing University in China to Boston University, where she earned her doctorate in Management. For decades, Guorong has refined her expertise in leadership development and talent management, delivering transformative solutions to organizations worldwide. Currently, Guorong holds a tenured professorship at Salem State University (Massachusetts), where she shares her knowledge and passion for management with aspiring students. Besides work, Guorong embraces life as a single mother, marathon runner, reader, writer, and gardener, finding balance, creativity, fulfillment, and joy in all pursuits.

About the Editors

Kimberly Kurzawa is a professional editor and owns Vital Ink, a freelance editing business that helps writers polish and proofread their work. She was born and raised in Vermont and now lives in Montpelier, enjoying the quiet and simple joys of life. When she isn't editing, Kimberly can be found at tea shops or taking long walks—preferably in nature and barefoot! She enjoys drinking tea as a mindfulness practice or with good company and deep conversation. You can find out more about her services at vital-ink.com.

Janet McKeehan-Medina grew up in Los Angeles and currently lives in New York with her husband. She's a trained psychotherapist and has always harbored a passion for writing. She feels writing can be very healing and incorporates creative activities in her sessions with clients. You may find her at www.janetmckeehanmedina.com.

Amy Place is a writer, editor, substitute teacher, library assistant, cook, and crossword puzzle enthusiast living in Vermont. She holds degrees in Liberal Arts and Literary Studies as well as certificates in Cosmetology and Professional Editing. If endlessly collecting degrees were a feasible pursuit, she would go for Linguistics, Graphic Design, Photography, Library Science, and more Literary

Studies, but for now she'll just continue reading lots of books. Find her at cafedisaffecto.substack.com.

Amy Quenneville lives in Vermont. She feels privileged to have participated as an editor for *Cold Lake Anthology 2024* and reviewed the hard work of so many authors.

Nancy Volkers is a professional medical and health writer, editor, and podcaster who works at home in rural Vermont amidst cats, chickens, and a tortoise named Bob. Nancy is the author of two novels—*A Scottish Ferry Tale* and *Scotland by Starlight*—and is working on a memoir. When not writing, she's usually at the gym, on a hiking trail, planning her next trip, or watching a documentary and eating ice cream. Find her on Substack at Seventy Thousand Thoughts (70000thoughts.substack.com).

Rebecca Wallick is a retired family law attorney, trail runner, and author currently living with her dogs in rural Vermont. Born and raised in the Seattle area, Rebecca spent 15 years living and running in Idaho's Salmon River Mountains before moving to Vermont in 2021. She is the author of *Growing Up Boeing: The Early Jet Age Through the Eyes of a Test Pilot's Daughter* (2014) and *Wild Running: Lessons from Dogs, Wolves, and the Natural World* (2024).

Acknowledgments

The Burlington Writers Workshop recognizes the hard work and commitment of the members of our writing community, who work with one another to refine and improve their writing craft. We acknowledge our workshop leaders for encouraging the artistic process, fostering collaboration and feedback in our writing groups, and providing a rich cultural forum for the literary arts. We thank the Burlington Writers Workshop Board of Directors and Leadership Team for their dedication and service to our community of writers.

Most especially, we appreciate the writers who have contributed to this year's anthology, and thank Charles Belson for the beautiful cover art.

www.ingramcontent.com/pod-product-compliance
Lightning Source LLC
Chambersburg PA
CBHW061218210726